DEFIANT SWORDS
BOOK TWO OF THE DURLINDRATH SERIES

Robert Ryan

Cover Design by www.bookcoverartistry.com

ISBN-13 978-0-9942054-4-5
(print edition)

Trotting Fox Press

I0458207

Contents

1. Brave Fool

Brand was at a loss. His enemies had him in a trap, and there was no way out. And yet, if he had the courage, there *was* a way. But it would take daring of a kind that did not involve swords or magic.

Khamdar stood tall and still. His pallid hands rested loose and confident on his wych-wood staff. He gave no hint of outward aggression, and yet a wave of malice, strong as a flood, flowed from him like a physical thing. Brand had heard of this before. It was said that the mere presence of one of the great sorcerers was enough to unman brave warriors. He believed it. And yet there was something in him that did not like to be pushed. The greater his fear became the stronger that thing inside him grew.

He felt the weight of the broken staff of Shurilgar in his hand. His whole purpose in retrieving it from the tombs was to destroy it, and thereby destroy its other half that was used by the enemy in their siege of Cardoroth. Anything less was a failure.

Yet Kareste looked at him, pleading silently, for she alone could use Shurilgar's staff with hope of defeating Khamdar.

The sorcerer, a brooding shadow, watched with malicious fascination. Dare he give it to her?

It was a good question, for it was now plain that Kareste had her own agenda, and if he gave her the staff he may never again have the chance to destroy it. If so, Cardoroth was doomed, and perhaps the whole land also, for he sensed that she teetered on the edge of becoming a sorceress. Khamdar had not lied when he claimed that.

One other choice Brand had, and he pondered it swiftly. He could take the staff back into the tombs and leave it there. He might survive the harakgar, the dark guardians of that shadow-haunted world, long enough to drop it into some bottomless chasm, for now that Kareste knew the charm that kept the harakgar at bay, she could retrieve it otherwise. Doing so, he might live, for as long as he did not attempt to take the staff out of the tombs the harakgar would probably not kill him. And there were other exits than the one he now stood before that would allow him to escape Khamdar.

But if he did any of that, Cardoroth would certainly fall, and likely Kareste also. His mistrust of her would surely push her closer to the enemies of the land.

He made his choice. There was no way to know if it was right, otherwise it would not have been so hard.

The ring of enemies behind Khamdar did not wait with the sorcerer's stillness. The Azan warriors gazed with hatred, their eyes dark slits, their hands tightly clenched about sword hilts. The elugs milled uncertainly, their iron-shod boots scraping the stone of the high ledge as they shuffled impatiently. From the beasts, the hounds born of dark sorcery, a low growl throbbed, deep and rumbling as though the earth moved and tumbled masses of stone into the abyss behind them.

Brand took a slow step back, and then another. All eyes watched him, even Kareste's, whose face showed at first surprise and then swift disappointment. She guessed his choice: he would not give her the broken remnant of Shurilgar's staff – instead he would return into the tombs of the Letharn behind him, preferring to dare its dangers rather than trust her with it.

He took another step and hoped that his instincts were right. Kareste studied him, understanding all that had just passed through his mind, or thinking that she did, for her face was stricken. The sight of her anguish stabbed him in the heart.

But she was wrong. The enemy now focused on him, which was what he intended, and they had forgotten her. With a sudden but sure motion he threw the staff to her. The black wood glinted, and its jagged ends of broken timber caught the light like flashing daggers.

Her eyes widened, but still her hand reached out, swift and sure as his own movement had been, and plucked the staff from the air.

Even as she did so, Brand voiced the Durlin creed.

Death or infamy! he yelled.

His voice rang clear and loud in challenge, but he did not wait for any answer. Instead, he leapt forward and struck out, aiming for Khamdar. If he destroyed their leader those who followed might falter. So he hoped, for no matter his skill at arms he could not defeat them all. He could not even defeat Khamdar alone, but his attempt might give Kareste the time she needed to decide what she was going to do – if she had not already fallen to the lure of dark sorcery.

But Brand did not use his skill at arms. He sensed that Khamdar was beyond such attacks, warded by arcane power. Instead, he drew on the newfound, unwanted, but desperately needed strength of magic that he had discovered within himself.

Blue-white flame spurted to life and ran along the oaken staff that Aranloth had given him. It flared and fluttered, then streaked toward the sorcerer.

Khamdar, poised and sure of himself, made a smooth motion with his own dark staff and waved Brand's attack aside without effort, diverting it harmlessly into the chasm that ran behind him.

Brand tried again, but even as he summoned flame Khamdar knocked the staff from his hand. It clattered over the stone as it fell, and Brand stood unprotected before the sorcerer.

At that moment he felt the full power of Khamdar, of one of the great elùgroths, and it chilled the blood in his veins. Fear surged through him, overwhelming dread that drove into him and urged him to run, to run anywhere to escape, even over the ledge and into the abyss, for surely such terror could not be endured.

He tore his gaze from the sorcerer and looked at Kareste. Her hands gripped tight the broken staff of Shurilgar, but she had not moved. Her face seemed strange, as though she summoned some great power, but he saw no sign of any spell. He did not understand what she was doing, but he saw no indication that she made any move to help him.

He gritted his teeth and planted his feet firmly on the ground. He was not going to run anywhere, no matter the shadow of madness that the sorcerer cast over him. If he must die, he would die fighting.

Khamdar laughed softly. He seemed perfectly at ease, confident that he could kill his prey whenever he chose, no matter that it tried to fight back.

Brand trembled. Despite the cloud of horror that deepened over him, that drained both strength and will, he slowly drew his sword.

The sorcerer grew still. His laughter ceased, and Brand drew assurance from the fact that his enemy seemed surprised.

The Halathrin-forged blade glittered and flickered in Brand's hand. A cold light seemed to shine within it.

Brand shook off a little of the fear that clung to him like a fog.

"You can kill," he said slowly to the elùgroth, "but you cannot win."

Brand was surprised at the steadiness of his voice, and his final choice was made, as he always made it: live or die; win or lose – he would fight.

He took a pace forward, and it required an enormous effort. Yet in doing so it freed him, for the fear that gripped him fell suddenly away, and despair and mad terror vanished with it. All that was left was a soaring will to defy the person who would oppress him, and in that moment, life and death, his quest, and the fate of Alithoras itself were all forgotten. There was only one thought, and that was to resist his enemy.

A shadow of doubt crossed the elùgroth's features, and his fingers flexed uncertainly on his wych-wood staff. Brand understood intuitively that it had been many long years since anyone had dared to challenge him. But whatever misgivings the sorcerer had, he swiftly stifled them, or else confidence in his unassailable might rose once more to the surface. He smiled, and then stepped forward himself.

An unexpected roaring filled Brand's ears. If it was some attack of sorcery, he did not understand it. But judging from how the elùgroth tilted his own head to listen, it was a surprise to him also.

And then suddenly Brand felt rough hands on him from behind. Kareste was there; he knew her by the flick of ash-blond hair that he saw from the corner of his eye. With a strength that he scarcely believed, she spun him around toward the cave and threw him to the ground. Taken by surprise and unprepared, he fell hard and tumbled awkwardly across the ancient stone ledge.

He had made a mistake – the greatest of his life. Kareste would side with the enemies of Alithoras, perhaps even rejoin the two halves of Shurilgar's staff, and the woe that would come of that was unthinkable, yet he must think of it, for it would be his fault.

A voice cracked at him like a whip. "Back, you fool! Back!"

It was Kareste. Her eyes were wild, and immense strain showed on her face. He staggered to his feet near the entrance to the tombs.

Kareste leaped back to join him, the broken staff of Shurilgar raised high. A moment Khamdar paused, uncertain of what was happening.

The roaring grew louder. Brand stood next to Kareste. He held his sword before him but was unsure where to face or what to do. From just behind he felt the stale breath of the tombs, and he sensed the harakgar stir within the tunnels that they guarded. A shiver ran up his spine, and the hair on the back of his neck prickled.

Khamdar made to move forward. The band that he led followed in his wake. But in midstride the sorcerer paused once more. This time he looked up, a wary expression on his face. The roar grew unbearably loud. A thrum ran through the ground.

Without warning Khamdar turned and fled through the ranks of his own followers. An Azan warrior, not quick enough to get out of his way, was blasted by crimson flame and propelled to the side in smoke and screams. At that moment white froth flew through the air above. It was followed by a spray of water and then a flood that tumbled and roared and raced in an avalanche of fury.

Kareste had called forth water from the river that ran above the tombs and drawn it to the ledge. The band of enemies screamed and panicked. Yet before they could move Brand saw many swept away over the ledge and into the abyss. Moments later all were lost from sight in the mighty torrent that gathered pace, sweeping rocks and smashing boulders before it.

Water-spray lashed Brand's face. The ledge before him trembled, and he was sure that some was taken away. He feared that Kareste had called too much water and that the whole platform of stone might crash and topple into the abyss, and they might yet be forced back into the caves, if even that was safe from collapse.

2. Evil must be Fought

The ledge groaned and the water roared. Rocks and boulders tumbled over the precipice, tearing and ripping away at the lip as though it were mere cloth. Yet as quickly as the water came, the great flood ceased.

Brand looked for any sign of their enemies. His searching gaze first took in the ruined edge of the platform, broken and tattered along its length, and then closer in where rubble and deep layers of silt had settled. Water trickled across the surface in little streams, draining into the abyss.

The ancient stone marker remained as it had for years beyond count, though its inscribed sides now glistened darkly with moisture. All these things he saw, but of the hunters who had pursued them from Cardoroth to the tombs of the Letharn, there was no sign.

Brand shivered, for the air was chill. It was as though the enemies who had stood there just moments ago had never existed. The force of Kareste's magic had swept them into oblivion. He had seen her use power before this, but not to such a catastrophic end. Her claim was true: she could use Shurilgar's staff. And though that had just now saved them, yet also its lure would draw her very soul into jeopardy.

He sat down on the stone, exhausted and uncaring of the wet surface. Kareste remained standing, gazing out into the abyss. There was an expression on her face that might have been elation, but there were times when he could not read her, and this was one. What she was thinking, he could not even guess, but certainly she gripped the black staff hard, as though she would never let it go, and that worried him.

After a while her fingers relaxed, and she glanced down at him.

"Don't think that they're all gone," she said. "We'll have trouble from them yet, before the end."

Brand looked out toward the chasm. "Surely nothing could survive that."

Kareste closed her eyes. "I no longer sense Khamdar, but that doesn't mean he's dead. He may have reached safety. Or, even if swept away by the flood, he might have survived it. Elùgroths are hard to kill. Harder than lòhrens, for they use their power all the time to ward themselves against the chances of the world."

Brand groaned and stood. It seemed that every muscle in his body ached, and even sheathing his sword hurt him.

He walked past the horses, huddled and scared near the wall, and gave them some reassuring words and a rub along their withers to help steady them. As he did so, he noticed that the rockfall that had once blocked the downward route along the ledge was gone: the flood had cleared it away, yet the stone cliff above remained blackened where the fire of some previous battle scorched it.

Brand moved cautiously to the broken edge and looked into the abyss. Kareste joined him. They gazed in silence, for below them was a scene of death. The bodies of their enemies were at the bottom of the gorge. Some floated, tugged back and forth in the ebb and flow of the receding floodwaters. Others, the tattered remnants of creatures that once walked, lay sprawled and broken on hard rocks.

"Better them than us," Kareste said.

Brand did not answer. Her comment was true, and yet it was not a sentiment that he would have voiced himself.

They stepped back from the ledge. "They're not all there," she said. "Perhaps some escaped, or maybe we just can't see all of the bodies. The rest may be obscured by water or swept away."

"There's no way to know for sure," he said. "Yet I admit that I'd feel more at ease if we'd seen Khamdar down there."

"He was quick to flee, sensing what was coming before the others. And he is warded also. He may be injured. Or he may be dead, but I doubt it."

"He's definitely not easy to kill," Brand said.

She raised an eyebrow. "Nor are you. That much I've learned for myself, though Aranloth evidently knew it before me."

Brand looked at her, drawn as always to her green-gold eyes, but unsure how well he knew her, if he knew her at all. And yet the risk he had just taken, enormous as it was, had paid off. They were safe, at least for the moment.

"What now?" he asked.

Kareste gazed back at him, her face masking the many things that she must have felt.

"First," she said, "Tell me why you gave me the staff. I didn't think you would."

Brand shrugged. "Honestly, I'm not sure myself. But what has been done to the Halathrin is a great evil. It cannot go unchallenged – it must be fought."

"So too must the siege of Cardoroth, but that continues. Yet you gave me the staff, and you must know that it occurs to me to keep it."

Brand shrugged again, but gave no answer.

She kept looking at him, her gaze intense. "You *trusted* me to give it back, but I don't know why."

"I pick my friends carefully," he answered. "And my quests also. If we stick together, we might both yet live. And may the king forgive me, but I agree that the

Halathrin, entrapped by sorcery as they are, must be freed. How can I decide to help only Cardoroth or to help only the Halathrin? It's in our power to attempt both, but it's a heavy burden to stand here knowing that my first quest is achieved – that I could destroy Shurilgar's staff and save Cardoroth – and yet not do it."

Kareste continued to look at him, and though her face showed nothing, he guessed at the turmoil that battled across her mind.

Her face did not change, but suddenly she held out the staff to him.

"We all pick our friends carefully. Or at least we try to."

For just a moment some great emotion welled to the surface, and her face flushed. But then she pushed it down and became the perfect picture of a lòhren again: calm, poised and tranquil.

"Take it," she said. "Khamdar was wrong. I'm no elùgroth, though I feel the lure of elùgai."

The staff shimmered darkly between them. He saw how hard it was for her to return it, though she nearly hid that from him. And he admired that she had the strength to offer it back, for surely if she kept it great power was at her command.

He saw also, more clearly than she, that her final choice of Light or Shadow, of lòhrengai or elùgai, was not yet made. From the moment that he took the staff from her, she would yearn for it. From the moment it was destroyed, which he still planned to do as swiftly as the Halathrin were freed, she would regret her choice. The blush of great power was on her, and its lure was strong, but so too was the freshness of her gratitude for his trust in her. But those opposing forces would wax and wane over time, the first growing stronger and the second receding.

She was not ready to make her choice, and to force the issue now might be to jeopardize her soul. For once a

13

person walked beneath the Shadow it was near impossible to turn around again. But if she could do it, it must be done in her own time and of her own will.

Yet still he hesitated amid a wave of doubt, for if he did not take the staff now and destroy it, then the risk to Cardoroth would grow, and with it the peril to the rest of Alithoras.

What would Aranloth want him to do? The knowledge that there were Halathrin, caught by foul sorcery and turned into beasts that roamed the world at the will of elùgroths, would tear at the lòhren's heart. And that the elùgroths did this, Khamdar chief among them, was not just a matter of spite or malice. There was a plan behind it.

He made his final choice. Even Cardoroth was a small thing compared to the fate of Alithoras. But he felt alone, for he was making decisions that even lòhrens and kings would find hard.

Aranloth had warned him that at all costs the staff must be destroyed as soon as it was brought from the tombs. Otherwise, it was at risk of being obtained by the enemy, and the damage they could cause with it was incalculable. But he must take up the burden of choice – there was no one else to do so.

He shook his head.

"Keep it," he said. "We go to the hills of Lòrenta to free the Halathrin, or to try to. But we must go there swiftly and destroy the staff when our quest is done."

Kareste looked at him strangely, and then slowly lowered her hand. She gripped the staff fiercely.

"I thought you would take it," she said.

He flashed a grin at her.

"So did I. But my choice is made, may the king forgive me, and it's behind me now. All that matters is to get to

Lòrenta quickly, but I fear that Khamdar waits for us above. He, and any of the band that survived with him."

"That may be," she said. "But another way, an old way has opened."

She pointed to where the rockfall had been cleared away. The downward path, though steep and narrow, seemed passable. "Taking it we can avoid Khamdar, for a time, but it will take us longer to get to Lòrenta. If we go that way it will take us into the Angle and we must cross rivers. And no doubt we will meet other dangers that we don't foresee."

"The new way might be safer," he said. "But the old way – back the way we came – will be swifter. And we're in need of haste."

"But however fast we get there," she answered, "we must still get there. The slower way offers a better chance of that. And not all the hunt was gathered here with Khamdar. We'll surely meet with the rest if we go back that way."

Brand sighed. "The delay chafes me, but what you say is true. We'll take our chances on the new road."

They mounted and looked around one last time. Brand would not be sorry to leave here. He still felt the presence of the harakgar, furious but muted within the tombs, and he knew he was lucky to have escaped.

The path ran steeply. The rockfall was gone, blasted away by the force of water that had flowed down the ledge like a river, but the stone was wet and treacherous, and it was no place to slip; the abyss opened to their left like a yawning mouth.

Kareste went first, leading her horse by hand. Brand did not like the Angle at all; everything that he had seen so far stank of death. Yet he wondered if it had always been like that. The great carvings on the cliff opposite the chasm told him that there was more to the Letharn than he had seen so far.

They continued downward, moving with caution. Kareste paused often, as though probing with some secret sense the state of the stone beneath their feet.

"It's perfectly safe," she said.

Brand was less sure. "Then why are you being so careful?"

She grinned at him but gave no answer.

Nothing, and no one, followed them, but the roar of the waterfalls, of the mighty river pouring down the escarpment just ahead of them, grew louder every moment.

As they went Brand studied the view. The Angle was visible between the two silver bands of river that bordered it. It was a green and lush land that swelled into a smooth-sloped hill toward its middle, but it was far away and hard to see properly. There were, perhaps, buildings on that rise, covering its crest and stretching down its long sides. If so, they were decrepit, barely more than rubble, but it was hard to tell though Brand strained his eyes. No doubt, if they were buildings rather than masses of broken and toppled boulders, they were the remnant of the city, or at least one of the cities, of the Letharn.

They neared the bottom of the ledge. There was water in the chasm below them, much closer now and still running from the flood Kareste had summoned. The broken body of an elug was caught between some upward thrusting rocks. Its head lolled at an unnatural angle, and flies gathered at its vacant eyes and open mouth.

Brand looked away. He took no joy in death, even of those who would kill him. But his thoughts soon turned to what lay ahead.

To their right was the face of the great escarpment, and over this thundered a mighty waterfall nearly a quarter of a mile wide. He had never seen anything like it.

Beyond, he saw the two rivers more clearly, for amid all the roar and spray of water this was the place where one river became two. Thus had the area earned the name of the Angle. But just before the Angle began, there was an island. A bridge spanned the first river and led to it, and then a second bridge spanned the next and led to other lands.

They rode ahead. Spray from the waterfall drove at them, and the horses became skittish. They crossed the first bridge and made the island. Water churned all around. Wind howled above, whipped up by the cascade of white water that smashed into stones, frothing and foaming.

Beneath the waterfall was a lake. From this sprang the two rivers. But the lake was not still and peaceful as was Lake Alithorin. Rather, it roiled and tossed in ceaseless motion.

They came to the second bridge. It was of ancient stone, pitted and marked by uncounted years, but it still had something of its original grace.

They crossed and worked their way through rocks and scree when they came to the other side. Brand was not sure there was a path, but Kareste seemed to have at least an idea of where she was going. Soon, a faded track became visible. It climbed the escarpment, winding to and fro. The horses slipped on loose rock and steep banks, sending sheets of scree sliding and clattering behind them, but they made progress, albeit slowly.

Eventually, they came to the top of the escarpment once more, but now on the opposite side of the river. Night was drawing on. It had been a long day, and they were exhausted.

To their right, some distance away, was a building. Brand saw it clearly, though clouds of fog rolled up at times from the falls. Ahead, the river flowed past, tree-lined and peaceful compared to what it became when it tumbled over the escarpment.

The building was of stone. It was an ancient thing, seeming lonely and deserted. It held something of the same grace as the bridges below. They did not ride past too closely, but Brand saw that it was constructed of granite blocks, each one at least as long and as high as a man. Its gray sides were dirtied by long years of fog, causing moss and lichen to grow thickly, and yet the building, the closer they approached it, gave off a feeling of awe. It had many strange windows, triangular slits in the stone.

The building itself was also shaped as a triangle, and massive entrances, triangular as well, stood open at each of its three sides. If there were any doors originally, they were long gone.

"What is it?" Brand asked.

"I don't know, but I sense danger there. Or somewhere beyond it."

Brand agreed, and as the sun set they left the escarpment and the strange building behind. There was something about it that disturbed him. Perhaps it was a feeling that beyond it waited the harakgar, though how he knew that, he could not be sure.

Night drew on swiftly, and the rush of the river dropped now to a smooth and steady flow, a faint and pleasant gurgle in the background.

They stopped to camp. They could go no further though all the hounds of the elùgroths were on their trail and an army of elugs to keep them company. But the land about them was still and peaceful, void of any obvious threat. Brand liked it. Yet it was still too dangerous to light a fire. Their enemies could be anywhere about, whether there was any sign of them or not. But neither was it cold, and no fire was needed.

They ate a simple and quick meal. And though they had not eaten in what seemed a very long time, they were not hungry.

Beside them was a small wood. Moths flew from it, and bats followed, wheeling and darting through the night. The stars were not bright; a haze filled the high airs and low clouds scudded, but they were not many and Brand did not think it would rain.

He liked woods, but he liked better being able to see and hear far into the distance. If their enemies came, he would have noticed from where they rested. And though he knew they should take turns to sleep, it was out of the question. No sooner had they finished eating than they lay down on the green grass, lush near the river, and sought the rest that only sleep could bring.

Yet for all Brand's tiredness, he slept poorly. Many times he woke. Once, sometime after midnight, a noise alerted him. A long while he listened, hearing a scuffling sound somewhere away in the dark, but it was only some small creature that sought worms or beetles on the verge of the wood.

The bats were gone. The clouds had disappeared, and the stars shone bright. It was cooler also, for a breeze played over the grassland and carried the nighttime scent of the river with it.

For a long while he did not get back to sleep, and he thought as he lay there, tossing and turning as the stars blinked at him and the creature wandered away in search of other food.

His thoughts turned at first to Kareste. He had been right to trust her, to give her the staff. Yet she was at risk, for the power in the talisman would call to her, but how else could she make her choice of Light or Shadow unless it was offered to her?

And when her moment came, as come it must, he intended to be there. Perhaps he could make a difference, as he saw now that Aranloth had tried to do when the other lòhrens would have had her expelled from their order.

At length, his thoughts turned to where they had shied away from all through the day. But now, in the deep night, where a man's troubles always rose to the surface of his mind, he could avoid it no longer. Aranloth had misled him. There was no real power in his staff. Brand knew that now. He realized also that Kareste had known the same thing from the moment they had first met, and had not meddled in Aranloth's affairs by stating it directly, though she had hinted at it.

Aranloth's staff was different to Shurilgar's. The broken staff was a relic, infused of old with enormous power, but with the lòhren's there was only the memory of enchantments worked through it, the bare traces of things that once were.

What power Brand had summoned had come from within himself. The thing that he most mistrusted in all the world was a part of him, inside him, at his very core. But why had Aranloth not told him that?

He felt a flicker of doubt at the lòhren's motives. And though what Aranloth had said could not be called a lie, it was bordering on it as close as was possible. He shrugged his misgivings aside, for he trusted Aranloth, and trust was easily eaten away by doubt. He would not doubt him, and he would not doubt Kareste either. They each had reasons for what they did, though it occurred to him with unexpected clarity that so too did Khamdar. In the sorcerer's own mind he was doing the right thing.

It was a startling realization, and it did not make Brand comfortable.

3. From Another World

Gilhain did not know what was happening, but he knew this much: Aranloth was right. Something was approaching; something wicked beyond the reach of thought.

The black-cloaked elùgroths sat in their wedge before the wall. Their wych-wood staffs pointed menacingly at the Cardurleth, and the rising chant of their spell smoked through the sorcery-laden air.

Beyond the wedge was the enemy host, and its multitudinous voice rose also in some eerie union with the invocation of the elùgroths, lending them power.

A wind blew, dry and hot, and then suddenly it changed. In what way, Gilhain could not be sure. It now smelled of moisture, or mold, or the decaying leaves of a forest that was thicker than any that grew near Cardoroth. But it was more than that.

"It comes!" hissed Aranloth.

Gilhain was sick to the pit of his stomach. He felt a great evil. It washed over him as did nausea to an ill man, in ever-greater waves that took him deeper into misery. Something was coming, and its arrival was inevitable. He could do nothing but wait.

He did not speak. Aranloth did not move. Soldiers waited all along the wall, and Gilhain knew that each and every one of them felt just as he.

The sun dimmed. The sky grew dark. The wind dropped, but the smell in the air intensified. It was putrid. He knew now that his guess was right. It was of a forest.

A wet forest. A forest layered deep by centuries of rotted leaves and mildew.

There was a growing sound also. It was an eerie thing, something over and above the world that surrounded him; he heard rain. Not just any rain – and certainly not the gentle nighttime rain that usually fell over Cardoroth, but a torrential downpour. It was a sound of watery fury, a sound that thrummed and boomed and lashed like a hundred storms gathering together and drawing near.

Gilhain looked around, confused. He did not know what was happening, nor did he understand why it grew suddenly hot. But hot it was, and more humid than he had ever felt before. The very earth before the Cardurleth began to steam.

Wisps of vapor rose sluggishly from the trampled earth. The gray tendrils twined about each other, swirling and undulating. His eyes followed them upward for a moment, and when he looked down again, he saw that the earth was gone. Where the ground had been, the same ground that he had known all his life and trod uncounted times, there was now a gaping void.

He saw at once that it was not quite empty. It seemed to be a valley, even if it had no place in Cardoroth. And within he saw a vague outline of steep banks, wind-lashed trees and cascading water.

But none of those things held his attention. Something else filled his vision, drew his gaze even though the horror of it was repellent.

A shape rose amid the steam. It flowed and writhed, but it was a thing of substance and not vapor. And it was massive.

He knew what it was, but his mind refused to accept what his eyes saw. It rose higher, reaching up and out of the void and into the air of Cardoroth.

"What is it?" he whispered to the lòhren. "How have they created such a sorcerous beast?"

Aranloth answered through gritted teeth. "This is not made of sorcery. Rather, it is called forth by the dark power of Shurilgar's staff. It is a beast, a real beast, but drawn from the otherworld, summoned from some dark pit of horror. It is a serpent, but one such as has never hunted any dim-lit forest of Alithoras."

Gilhain shook his head. "No. It can't be. No serpent ever grew so big."

"Not on *this* earth," Aranloth answered.

Up the serpent rose, swaying back and forth, yet ever its eyes, slitted pits darker even than the hollow from which it emerged, fixed on the Cardurleth – or those standing upon it.

"How shall we fight it?" whispered Gilhain.

"Nay," the lòhren said. "Men must fight men, and lòhrens must oppose dark sorcery. This task falls to my kind. It is for this that we came."

He stepped close to the edge of the battlement, a figure robed in white and clothed in determination, but a small and frail thing compared to what it faced.

Aranloth raised his arms, and all along the wall a dozen other lòhrens, apparently waiting for some such signal, lifted high their staffs.

The serpent rose higher still, and its shadow fell over the Cardurleth. It looked down upon the lòhrens and soldiers. Slime dripped from its pale belly. The scales that formed its skin were large and smooth, shimmering luminously from beneath but gleaming darkly along its top. Near its midsection was a massive bulge; the remains of what it had last eaten.

The chanting of the elugs reached a new height of frenetic madness. The drums beat wildly. But the spell of the elùgroths soared above all else, and yet gathered all in and drew it into its own power, shaping it to its own dark will.

On the battlement, all was still and no sound was made. Men flinched when the shadow of the serpent touched them, but they made no cry of fear. Though terror menaced them, they held their ground; the longer the siege endured, the greater their defiance grew.

Gilhain gave a signal. Perhaps this attack was beyond mortal strength, but that did not mean the soldiers could not attempt to fight anyway. No one should just meekly await their fate.

A carnyx horn sounded at the king's gesture, and its deep-throated voice sent a command to every captain along the wall. And they in turn gave their own commands.

Within moments the air was dense with arrows – the red-flighted arrows for which Cardoroth was famous. They whistled as they flew, blazing through the air like a spray of blood. But when they struck the massive serpent they shattered or glanced away. Some few stuck, but they did not penetrate the thick scales into the softer flesh beneath. The creature ignored the attack, swaying ever higher.

The next volley of arrows flew. These were better aimed, seeking the two places that were likely more vulnerable: where the great angular head joined the body, and the eyes.

Arrows stuck thickly in the skin at its neck, but they had no effect there. Those that struck the eyes seemed to trouble it, and it rose higher with a jerk, but then two great inner-lids, thick and leathery, came across from the sides. These offered protection, but seemingly no hindrance to its sight.

A ripple of movement ran through those on the battlement. Gilhain looked, but he did not at first see the cause, though he noticed a change. The men stepped back, but not in retreat.

It was only when the lòhrens took a pace forward that he realized the time for another type of attack had come. They would soon see if lòhrengai proved more effective than steel-headed shafts.

In unison the lòhrens raised their staffs. Aranloth reached forth with his hands. Lòhren-fire flared. A light, brilliant and flashing, sprang into being, dazzling and shimmering with its varied colors: silver, white, green, blue and many hues beside.

The lòhrengai struck the serpent, and the air all about it wavered with heat. Those who watched turned their heads away from the stabbing brightness. A moment later there was a crack as of thunder; it rolled and boomed, drowning out the drums of the enemy and their chanting. For long moments the noise throbbed, sending shivers through the rampart and deep into the earth. Light and thunder roiled over Cardoroth, and then slowly receded.

Gilhain lifted his gaze, but the serpent was still there.

"How is it *possible*?" he muttered.

Unaffected, the creature swayed higher. The arrows that had prickled its skin were now burnt away, and their ashes drifted like black snow through the air. The slime on its belly steamed, but the monstrous thing was unharmed, oblivious to the mighty power unleashed upon it.

Gilhain struggled to think of something to do, but he, the supposed strategist, the war-leader with a thousand tricks, was powerless and void of ideas. Truly, Aranloth was right. The serpent was from another world, for powers that would destroy a thing born of this earth were as nothing to it.

Aranloth looked ancient and weary, but he spoke with unexpected determination in the face of what had just happened.

"Long has been my battle against the Shadow," he said. "Mayhap it is ended, and Cardoroth with it. And yet know this, O king, the lòhrens will fight, no matter that they lose."

Gilhain knew it. He felt it in his bones. He looked around and sensed the same in the soldiers all along the wall. They would fight. Every one of them would carry their blades until the end. But if lòhrengai had not harmed the creature summoned to break them, nor swift-flighted arrows shot from strong bows, then swords would not either, no matter how defiant.

"The great dark is coming," he answered slowly. "Yet now I feel better about sending Brand on his quest. He at least has a hope of life, and it may be a long time before the same darkness overshadows him."

4. A Haunted Man

Brand grappled with the thought of the power that was in him. He wanted no part of it, and vowed at some point during the night not to ever use it again. Lòhrengai was for lòhrens, and he was a warrior. Besides, he mistrusted it for good reason. Magic changed the wielder. It used them even as they used it. For a lòhren less so than an elùgroth, because they invoked the art only at need, but that was beside the point. He wanted to stay just as he was.

Aranloth knew. He knew the dangers better than any, and he had known that hidden away somewhere inside Brand that power lurked. At least he guessed it. But Brand did not really blame him for saying nothing. Just as he himself knew that Kareste faced a great choice, and that such choices must be discovered and faced by the person, in their own time. Pressure from outside only got in the way.

Dawn came after a long night. Brand's choices were made, though he supposed they would yet be tested. But he thought no more of magic or problems or the dark corners of a man's soul. Instead, he reveled in the new day.

The sun shone bright and clear. The sky was a glorious blue, and the grass was green beneath the hooves of the horses as they got underway. Afar, he heard the gurgle and rush of the river, and closer to hand the calls of many types of birds that he had never heard before. But he could not see them, for they came from within the many small woods that dotted the landscape.

The horses travelled quickly. It was good country in which to ride, the earth being soft and the way clear of obstacles. All should be well, Brand thought, and yet Kareste was withdrawn and thoughtful.

He considered her as they rode. At first, he guessed her state of mind was because of Shurilgar's staff. After some while though, he realized that was not the case. He began to feel something himself, something which she had sensed earlier than he: a mood of unease that lay over the land despite the beautiful day. It was not strong. It was, in fact, barely there. But he had learned to trust his instincts, and now that they sensed this thing there was no doubt in his mind.

He caught her glance and they slowed the horses to a walk.

"What is it?" he asked.

"You sense it also? I thought it was just me."

"No," he answered. "There's something … not right. At first I didn't notice because the weather is so fine and this is a fair land. But there's something else going on."

Kareste gazed behind them. "Khamdar?"

"It could be," Brand said, following her gaze. "But there's no sign of any pursuit."

"Whatever it is, it's unsettling," Kareste said. She turned her gaze back to the front with an air of determination, and they continued on.

Now that their misgivings were in the open, their unease grew. It was like a shadow over the whole land, though they rode in bright sunlight.

They did not push the horses too hard. It was a long way to Lòrenta, and it was wise to keep them in good health and with a reserve of speed should it be needed. To tire them out now was to leave nothing available if they were pressed hard by a pursuit later.

Every moment that passed seemed like an eternity to Brand, but he pushed such thinking aside. To rush now might be a mistake, and he knew that although they did not hasten unduly, they were still making excellent time. Cardoroth could not endure forever, but he trusted in the king and the brave hearts of the city's people to hold out until the last. And by then, well, by then his own troubles would be sorted, one way or the other.

To their left was another wood. It was small, perhaps only a patch of five to ten acres, but it seemed green and lush as did everything in this land. He realized as they neared that no birdcalls came from it. But it was not silent.

Drifting through the sunlit air was music: high, wild, and laden with grief. It was a flute, that much Brand knew, but he had never heard such a tune before, and goosebumps stood out on his skin.

They came to a halt. "Who lives in these lands?" he asked.

Kareste frowned. "None that I know of. But Alithoras is large, and many people from the south are on the move. Maybe some have come here to escape trouble."

"If so, they'll be disappointed."

She looked at him, her eyes giving away nothing of her thoughts, but there was a catch in her voice.

"When people are desperate, even disappointment can be an improvement on their situation."

Brand did not answer. Kareste had suffered in her life, even more than he, so he took her at her word. He did not know what it would be like to lose his family as young as she had, and to be taken to some strange place among just as strange a people. At least he had stayed in his own land, moving from family to family, hiding spot to hiding spot, but always among his own kind who protected and taught him while the usurper of his father's chieftainship hunted for him.

Brand sighed. The past was a part of him, and he could not shake it any more than Kareste could distance herself from her own. But now he must force himself to think of only the present.

"Could it be a trap?"

Kareste shrugged. "Maybe, but I don't think so. It's not something that Khamdar seems likely to do, but there are other perils in the world beside elùgroths."

Brand made up his mind. "I would meet the person who could create such music."

"Curiosity is a dangerous thing," she said. "You like the music, but you may not like the maker. And it *may* be a trap, for all that I know."

"That's true, but it may also be a chance to hear news. We're wandering in a foreign land, and information helps. There could be elug armies on the move for all that we know."

She shrugged. "Very well. But be ready – for anything."

"Being ready is easy. It's making good choices that's hard."

She raised an eyebrow at him as though considering his words in a range of contexts, but did not speak.

They moved ahead. The wood was a little bigger than Brand had thought, but it was still small. Not so small that it could not hide an army of elugs if it came to that, but he did not really believe that to be the case. Khamdar must still be behind them somewhere, if he was even alive at all. And any enemy from the south was likely to be gathered around Cardoroth or one of the other cities along the coast of Alithoras. There was nothing for them here in the wild lands.

When the two riders entered the woods the light turned yellow-green. There were mostly oak trees about them, and the shade soon grew thicker. But it was a young wood, not so dense and dark as what Brand was used to.

They moved quietly, and with caution. But for all that they did not make any noise, the music died almost as soon as they rode beneath the leaf canopy, and it did not start again.

There was a path of sorts, though it veered at strange angles that no animal would make. But Brand was little skilled at tracking, and he was not sure of this. But however the path was made, he followed it, for it led to the center of the wood, and that was where the music had come from. So much he realized before it ceased. But whether the maker would still be there when they arrived was another matter.

A breeze whispered in the high leaves of the oaks, but it was still and peaceful amid the dark trunks and spreading boughs. The smell of the earth, deep and rich, was strong in the air and Brand liked it. It reminded him of the scent of new-ploughed soil, and not for the first time he missed his childhood home where once he had lived and toiled honestly, helping to raise livestock and crops for those who hid and protected him.

His past, his broken childhood, seemed a long time ago now. And yet it was not. But much had happened since then, and he had been forced to grow in strength and wisdom more quickly than he should have. Now, instead of crops, he harvested only death. Many were the enemies that he had left behind him. Sometimes, he wished for a simpler life. But then he would never have met Gilhain or Aranloth … or Kareste.

It was a mistake to allow his mind to continue wandering, and he focused his attention once more on the present. They neared the center of the wood. There was smoke in the air, the sweet-sharp odor that was a camper's friend. But not all campsites were friendly.

Brand brought his horse to a stop and looked around. He immediately saw the faint flicker of firelight from a glade a little ahead. The trees closed around it; the path passed to its side, but within the circle of trunks was a clearing: green-grassed and shining in the sun.

"Be careful," Kareste whispered.

He nodded, and urged his mount forward. The trunks were close, but not so close that a horse could not pass between them. On the inside, the light was brighter and the blue sky gleamed above.

It was a beautiful little glade, quiet and peaceful. The fire burned merrily in the middle, and to its side over a bed of black-red coals was a spitted hare, nearly roasted through. Behind that a magnificent black mare stood. She remained still, but occasionally an ear twitched or her tail lashed to dislodge flies. Against an ancient tree stump, thick but near-rotted by age, leaned a flute of black walnut, trimmed in gold. But of the flute's owner, the mare's rider and the fire's maker, there was no sign.

"Whoever it is has good taste in horses," Brand said.

There was a noise to the left of the glade and a man stepped from behind a tree trunk.

"There are few things in life better than a fast horse and sweet music," he said.

The man was tall and grim. He was also armed. He held a sword, finely crafted, in his hand, and he looked to Brand's trained eye like he knew how to use it, but he made no threatening move.

Brand thought quickly. He did not blame the stranger for drawing his blade in such a situation, but he did not draw his own. Instead, he ignored the naked steel. That would send a signal that he did not wish to fight, but also that he was not scared.

"To that," he answered, "I can only agree. But I would add this to it – a trusted sword ready to one hand, and a tankard of beer in the other."

The other man laughed. It was a deep and rich sound, but he did not lower his sword.

"You're a man after my own heart," he said.

Kareste sniffed loudly. "Enough of this. If I hear either of you say that the only other thing you need is a beautiful girl by your side, there's going to be trouble."

"My dear," the man said in his rich voice, "a beautiful girl is *always* trouble."

Kareste tossed her hair and glared at him. The man pretended not to notice and gazed back, a slightly impudent smile on his face.

Brand liked him. But then he felt an unexpected pang of jealousy. He did not know where it came from, and he did not like it.

The man looked from one of them to the other. With a nonchalant shrug, he lowered his sword.

"You're not one of my enemies," he said.

"Nor are you one of ours, I think," Brand answered calmly.

The man sheathed his blade. "But there's trouble nonetheless, and for once it's not of a kind that beautiful women bring." He ignored Kareste completely as he spoke, and she bit her lip, forcing herself not to react to his teasing.

He gazed at them a little longer. "But this you already know."

Brand nodded slowly, unsure of what to say, and thinking it best to say as little as possible.

"There are enemies behind us. Dangerous enemies. But we don't know for sure if they're still on our trail."

"I see," the man said. "Well, you seem able to look after yourselves; that much is obvious. So too is the fact that you tell me nothing that I couldn't already guess by your attitude. But that is no matter."

He turned to Kareste and gave a well-practiced bow. "My name is Bragga Mor."

Kareste sniffed again as a sign of irritation, though whether to the man as a person, or to his shrewd guesses, Brand did not know.

He gave the stranger their true names – there was no reason not to. In the pause that followed, he asked a question.

"Where are you from?" He had thought it a simple question, but Bragga Mor seemed suddenly to lose a little of his poise.

"It doesn't matter. I'm nothing but a vagabond wanderer now, and far I've travelled, and many things I've seen."

Brand was not going to press him on his home city. There was some darkness there, that much was obvious, but that the man had travelled was interesting.

"What have you seen?" he asked. "What passes in Alithoras?"

"Many things," Bragga Mor replied tiredly. "The enemy is now in the northlands. There are raging bands about, but, at least as I hear it, most are concentrated around Cardoroth. A vast army besieges that city." He gave Brand a questioning look, and Brand nodded without speaking. Bragga Mor seemed to need little else by way of confirmation. He was clever, and had already guessed where Brand had come from, and no doubt many more things besides.

The stranger continued. "There's rumor of dark deeds in the west. The eastern realms are nervous, knowing that trial of war may soon come to them, though as yet I have not heard that anywhere is attacked save Cardoroth. At least, that was the last I heard, but my news is old, for the wild lands call me now, and the works of men that do not last only haunt me. I avoid them."

Brand felt again that some darkness lay behind this man, and he was making his own guesses. But a sharp hiss from Kareste distracted him.

"Something comes!" she said.

Brand drew his sword and remained quiet, but into the silence Bragga Mor spoke.

"Of course," he said, turning to Kareste, "as you knew it must." He faced Brand again. "The very air sings with unease, and the beautiful girl knows why."

5. It Calls to the Dark

The two men looked at Kareste; one with apparent knowledge, and the other in surprise.

Kareste merely shrugged. "I did not know – I only guessed."

"But now you know that your guess is right," Bragga Mor said.

"They usually are," she answered. "But more to the point, how do *you* know?"

"Oh, I've seen a thing or two. Yes I have. More than I would like. Things to burn a man's vision and haunt his dreams. I know power when I see it – lòhrengai, elùgai and even ùhrengai, the force that forms and substances the world and from which both light and shadow spring."

"Is someone going to tell me what's going on?" Brand asked.

Kareste nudged her mount toward him. "Shurilgar's staff is a powerful thing. It calls. It calls to the Shadow, and the Shadow hears. I don't just mean the enemies that have hunted us, nor just Khamdar, if he still lives. I mean the dark things that dwell in Alithoras – the evil that lives in deep valleys, or lurks in the marshes, or haunts the forests and roams the lonely hills. The evil that hides; in short, all the shadowy creatures that have hated people since people first learned to kindle fire and keep the dark at bay."

"What does all that *mean*?" Brand asked.

"It means," replied Bragga Mor, "that you're in trouble. As the girl says, something comes. I have seen it. Or rather, I have seen *her*. A witch she is. I spotted her walking the starlit grasslands last night. To be sure, she is not one of the great ones, but she is still mighty powerful. And," he pointed at the broken half of Shurilgar's staff, "she would have more – more of what *that* can give to her."

Kareste did not seem disturbed. "How do you know that she isn't one of the great ones?"

"I've seen one of them," he said. His voice trailed away and his gaze became distant.

Brand had heard enough. "It's time to go," he said, "And quickly."

Bragga Mor looked at him sharply. The past obviously troubled him, but he could give his attention to the present swiftly enough if he chose to.

"No. You cannot flee her. You must stay and fight, if it comes to that. Better to face her now than at some point in the future when you may be less able."

Brand thought quickly. There was something to what Bragga Mor said. Who knew what the future held? And if the witch joined forces with Khamdar, then the situation would become much worse.

"Will you fight with us?" Brand asked. He knew nothing of this stranger, and the man had no reason to help. But there was something about him…

"Or," Kareste cut in, "Will you fight with the witch?"

Brand had not thought of that as a possibility, but immediately on her words he wondered if his own instincts were wrong.

Bragga Mor looked at her and smiled. "That, we shall see."

Brand cocked his head and listened. A change had come over the wood. He could not quite name what it was, but it seemed as though even the leaves at the tops of the trees were hushed, and the trunks were still like an army of wary men that silently watched an approaching messenger, unafraid of him, but fearing the import of his tidings.

The witch came. One moment she was not there, though her presence filled the wood, and then she was among them, seeming to coalesce from the shadows at the fringe of the clearing into flesh and blood that stepped upon the grass.

Brand was ready. He maneuvered his mount to face her, but he did not put his back to Bragga Mor.

She that had come was light-footed, for her steps quickly took her to the middle of the glade, but she moved without haste or sign of threat. And it was a strange thing to see how she elegantly walked, for judging by her appearance, it seemed to Brand that she should have hobbled.

The witch was old. Her skin hung on her in wrinkled folds that swung as she moved. Her hair, a mess of long gray strands and wisps of white, fell over her narrow shoulders and down her hunched back. Her nose, long and hooked, jutted forward like a bird's beak. Above it, glaring like a hawk's, her eyes held each of their own in turn. There was no sign of frailty there, despite her decrepit body and her ancient, ugly face.

She raised an arm. The tattered remnants of robes fell back, revealing more withered skin. A crooked finger, dirty-nailed and swollen at the joints, pointed at Kareste.

"I know what it is that you carry," she said.

Her voice confused Brand. It was smooth and clear and beautiful: the voice of a woman in the flower of her youth.

Though the voice surprised him, he perceived instinctively that her power resided in it. It was a voice to command, to persuade, to inspire trust. Most of all, it was a voice that could carry and enhance spells. And spells he would be wary of, for she had come to take Shurilgar's staff, and she would not be idle in pursuing that goal.

Her words to Kareste were not loud, but they seemed to fill the clearing and to echo strangely up and down the shadowy aisles of tree trunks.

Kareste quivered with emotion. "Stay back, hag. Or die."

Brand looked on silently. Bragga Mor did not move. Surprisingly, the witch showed no anger. She gazed at Kareste calmly, her hawk-like eyes gleaming with humor.

"By that," she replied, "you mean 'don't try to take the staff, or I'll fight to the death to keep it.' Has it already got such a strong hold on you?"

Kareste stiffened, but the witch went on speaking. "You are young in your power. I am old. Old as the hills and wily as the ancient beasts that roam them, seldom seen by man. I have many names. Hag is one. Slithrest, Netherwall and Angrod are others. Those names were old before even the Halathrin strode ashore to this land."

The witch straightened, and a hard edge of threat came into her voice. "But they named me Durletha – enduring as stone. And that should be a warning to you, for I have seen frost break mountains into plains and flat plains themselves raised into high mountains. I have seen the great sea, black and terrible beyond the reach of your thought, climb the shore and sweep all before it. I will be here when it comes again. I have seen the bright Halathrin, proud and stern and aloof. I watched unmoved as they came, and I looked on uncaring as they dwindled. I saw the Letharn rise before them, whose lands you are passing through, whose lands you would still be passing through though you rode for weeks, and I saw them fall. And before them were the Kirsch, whom men have forgotten. So, foolish girl, will you contend with me?"

It was Brand who answered. "She is not alone."

Durletha turned her fierce eyes upon him. "Ah. You speak at last. You are younger than she, but perhaps wiser." The witch frowned for a moment, assessing him. "Yes, I see it now. There is no give in you. You will fight for her. But will you *die* for her?"

"No one needs to die today," he said.

She paused, continuing to look at him intently. "But death follows you, does it not?" she said after a moment. "Everywhere you go. Even in Red Cardoroth, that will fall in blood and flame. And who protects you? You think you protect the king, but the king is protecting you, else you would be dying with him even as we speak."

Brand showed nothing of what he felt at those words. Durletha seemed to know far too much about what was happening. That she had some measure of Sight was evident, but that did not mean she was not lying.

Her gaze did not leave him, but her haggard face broke into a grin and she clapped her hands.

"Yes, you're wiser than your companion. She shall surely fall at the end, but you, you might yet stand tall. Yes, even without me you could command armies, wear a crown and conquer wide realms. But with *me* at your side, we could rule all of Alithoras. The petty lòhrens and the shadow in the south would fight each other for the crumbs under our table. Yes, it could be so."

Brand raised his eyebrows but did not speak. He had heard this kind of thing before from those with the Sight, but not from one so old and decrepit – not from one who would make him her paramour.

"And you are polite, too. But I have more pleasing forms than this!"

The forest remained still, but birds now sang in the dappled sunlight. A sweet breeze blew, carrying the scent of earth, leaf and flower, and some exotic perfume that he could not name.

41

"I am not of the Light," she said softly. "But neither am I of the Shadow."

"Are you not?"

"No. But I can be anything between them!"

The sun now seemed dazzling bright in the clearing. Bright beams shot amid the trees and Brand raised a hand to shield his eyes.

As quick as the stabbing light came it disappeared. When it was gone, the witch stood just where she had been, but she was transformed.

Durletha was now young, and it seemed to Brand that it was no spell but her true form. Her hair was long, flowing in golden locks that shimmered like burnished metal. Her skin was smooth and unblemished, seeming to glow with health and beauty. Nor did she stand bent and hump-backed, but tall and proud. She gazed at him with a cool look, a look of utter confidence, but yet from the same hawk-like eyes as before.

And with a shimmer she changed again. This time she appeared as Kareste, but it was a Kareste that he had never seen before. In form, the likeness was identical, but there was a sweet smile on her lips, and a grace in the way she stood that spoke of gentleness and care, not of a strong sword arm and a sharp tongue. This time also her eyes had changed: they were green-gold, and they laughed at him with a carefree joy.

"I can be anything you want," the witch said. "Anything." And her voice was Kareste's, but it contained a promise of intimacy that he had never heard in it before.

"I can be anything you want, and the world will be ruled by your sword, and by your will."

Brand hesitated, and then he grinned back at her boyishly. She had made a mistake. She spoke of realms and armies and swords. She spoke of war and conquest and rule, but she made no mention of the staff he bore or

42

of the power that was in him, and that told him what she most feared and least wished him to consider.

He gripped Aranloth's staff tightly. It was warm to his hand. He felt the residue of lòhrengai within it. That force called to him, and he felt it all around him also.

The forces that formed and substanced the world were everywhere, and he was becoming more sensitive to them. He knew now that he could summon them, transform them, use them. That ability was in him, but in bringing those forces into himself they would change him even as he changed them.

And each time he used such power he would become more adept. He would sense the call more strongly. Each step he took down that road was a step that he could never retrace. Once followed, there was no turning back from the path ahead. And in following it, it would alter him forever, and perhaps not for the best.

Dare he try to use such power one last time? And what of his vow? Could he so easily break it, even if need drove him? They were hard questions, and he had no answers. But at the same time he sensed that the choice was before him. The witch had made it so, and she had no fear of his sword. That much was clear.

There was little time left. That Durletha would try to claim the staff was obvious. It was equally obvious that she must not have it. To that end, he would fight. But how?

She did not fear his sword. To what extent she feared lòhrengai, he could not tell. But she was far more skilled in such things than he. If he used it, she would defeat him easily. And yet there was Kareste also. She would fight, and between the two of them they might defeat her. But if he joined Kareste in that, he would become what he did not wish, what he least trusted.

43

Still he stood, undecided, and the brief moments flitted by. Soon the witch would realize that her attempt to persuade him had failed, and then she would attack.

But he was caught in a dilemma that he could not solve. And a new thought struck him as a blow, and disabled him.

Why should he not embrace his new-found power?

6. An Iron-hard Will

The great serpent rose higher, a massive thing that even those in distant parts of Cardoroth could see. People ran into the streets; some screamed, others remained deathly quiet, watching.

Gilhain, atop the battlement, was one who watched in silence. The creature's coils flowed and undulated, ascending from the vast pit without end.

It towered above the Cardurleth, blotting out the sun. But it did not strike. Gilhain realized that it would not attack that way; it would not rend with its great fangs or use poison. It had some other means to visit destruction upon them.

The creature's lower portions began to slide along the rampart. It covered hundreds of feet of stonework, grinding and smashing against the merlons, sending them tumbling down in ruin to the earth below.

Though the coils were thicker than the trunk of an ancient oak, the soldiers attacked. Their blades did nothing. Some of them, getting too close, were crushed by a sudden heave of the serpent. The stones ran red with blood.

With its slow haste, the serpent continued, oblivious to the hundreds of men that attacked it like a swarm of ants.

A stench filled the air, and Gilhain and his wife gagged at the putrid smell. Slime dripped down the stone. Aranloth stood close by, unaffected. His head was down, either in acceptance of an opponent beyond his ability to fight, or else in deep thought.

"May fate show us mercy," whispered Aurellin.

The great loops of the serpent began to constrict. They closed slowly, but surely. Stone popped. Sprays of dust and loose gravel filled the air. Cracks appeared, not just in merlons but lower down. A deep grinding noise thrummed through the air and pulsated up through the stone into Gilhain's feet.

He took Aurellin's hand in his own. "It will bring down the Cardurleth," he said softly.

"And let in the horde," she answered.

They watched in terrible fascination as a white-robed lòhren, near the head of the beast, made a desperate move. Her black hair spilled out behind her as she ran. Swift she moved, but the creature paid no heed. And then she was upon it, thrusting her staff into its mouth.

Purple-blue lòhrengai flared. Men with axes raced behind her, attacking in unison. They hewed with mighty swings at the neck, as near as they dared approach the flame.

The creature made no sound, but a ripple ran through it. Suddenly, it threw up coils of its long body. They crashed into the men and sent them sprawling, axes clattering from lifeless hands. Some few crawled away, broken bones slowing them, but they escaped.

The lòhren was not so lucky. Bravely she stayed where she was, lòhrengai flaring from her staff until she dropped to her knees, exhausted. But the great jaws of the beast snapped shut around her.

She screamed. Blood sprayed. Bones snapped with a crack audible even to Gilhain. Her staff fell from her writhing arms. The creature then spat her out, its massive jaws agape, and the ruined body of the lòhren fell, tumbling across the rampart and down the other side into the city streets.

Wider still the jaws opened, and the beast vomited the lòhrengai back out. It seemed unharmed.

The screaming of the city folk was a sound such as Gilhain had never heard before, nor ever wanted to hear again. It was primal fear given voice, unfettered by thought or hope or restraint. Other cities had heard it, other cities that had fallen before the enemy. But they had not fallen without a fight; they had not gone willingly under the shadow, and nor would Gilhain.

Without word or gesture or haste, the king drew his sword. He stepped forward to attack, and men followed him. It was no longer about hope of victory; it was about fighting an enemy, about never surrendering to an opponent. Blades would not work. Lòhrengai would not work. But that did not mean he would not try to the last, and there was a victory in that worth more than life. It *was* life, for nothing else mattered in the end.

The great sword of the king hacked and slashed. The soldiers near him did the same. Yet for all their effort they were like men hewing at a mighty oak with paper axes: the scales of the serpent were too thick and the blows were as nothing.

The massive coils of the serpent rose above the king. The queen now leaped to his side, stabbing with a knife, and the shadow of the creature fell over them. Whether by accident, the intelligence of the creature, or the design of the elùgroths who had summoned it, the coils crashed down seeking to crush them both.

But the Durlin were there. In a last great effort they flung themselves forward, some to attack the creature with pikes, others to pull back the king and queen to safety. Some died beneath the toppling coils, crushed and broken, but the king and queen were saved, the pikes holding back the weight of the monster for just a moment before they slipped away beneath its vast bulk.

More stone popped, and powdery dust filled the air. Rubble fell. The foundations of the Cardurleth shook. The coils gripped ever tighter, yet no one fled.

Gilhain stumbled back. This was it. This was the fall of Cardoroth. He was powerless to stop it, and the prophecy of old, the foretelling of destruction that had come down through the long years was correct: the city would fall in red fire and blood.

Cold fear stabbed him. Despair smothered him. His own life would soon end also, and that of his wife. Ruin would take them all.

He held out a hand to Aurellin, and she took it. They did not speak. No words were necessary. All that mattered was that they would be together when the end came.

He drew his gaze away from the person he loved most in the world, and looked to Aranloth. He would say goodbye to one of his great friends. But the lòhren did not look at him. Instead, he strode forth.

Aranloth lifted his arms high, and there was a look of such determination on his face that the king's heart skipped a beat. The lòhren would not yield. His was a will beyond a normal man's; a will honed and strengthened by forgotten ages. He was like a force of nature, and his heart's beat was one with the life of the land that he had wandered for years beyond count.

The lòhren spoke no word. He gave no sign. And yet every other lòhren along the rampart instantly looked at him. Something passed between them, between the students and the master. If it were possible, the expression on his face of iron-hard will strengthened further. It was a will that had seen ages of men come and pass. He was a thing of the land itself – old as the hills, bearing a burden of time and change even as did they. And he had learned a thing or two in that time. He had survived.

Gilhain watched, awed and puzzled. What would the man he dared to call a friend do?

7. The Flicking Wings of a Hawk

"You cannot tempt me," Brand said. "I want neither realms nor armies. I want nothing you offer. Stand aside. You have no claim on the staff."

The witch smiled at him sweetly. Her glance was long and keen and intimate. With a sudden stab he knew that he wished to see that same look on the real Kareste.

"Begone!" he said.

She tossed her ash-blond hair. "In life you often get what you don't want, though few say no to realms or armies – or even magic."

It disturbed Brand how much she knew of him, how much she read from his mind. Some things were easy to guess, but others were not. Hers was a peculiar magic, but all magics had strengths and weaknesses. He would discover her weakness in due course, and to that end he did not mind talking. It would give him time.

She smiled at him. It was a smile for him alone as though no one else in the world mattered.

"I know what it is that you most want. A simple thing it is too. You wish to inherit what should have been yours – the chieftainship of the Duthenor. You already wear the helm on your head, and the sword of your forefathers is always by your side. But an usurper rules in your place, supported by men from other tribes, and he will not be easy to dislodge. Yet it would be a small thing for me to accomplish. For you, I could do it. I could do it with ease. And you should know this, also. The usurper will one day be usurped himself. The wild men that he has brought in will turn on him, and in the end they will rule the Duthenor. And they will be harsh masters."

Brand was troubled, and this time he could not disguise it. Not that it would be worth the effort to try; Durletha seemed to know more about him than he did himself. Worse, she seemed to know his very thoughts.

"Begone!" he said again. "Temptation will not sway me, and fate will be what it will be."

For the first time, the witch showed displeasure. And in that Brand took hope, for it seemed to him the only reason she had to be displeased was that her offers were rejected. Yet, if she truly knew his innermost thoughts, she would have known from the beginning that it would be so. He was loyal, if nothing else, and Gilhain, and now Kareste, were his friends. No force on earth, and no temptation, would cause him to break trust with them.

Durletha hissed. It was a frightful sound, and it was all the stranger to now see open hatred on the mask of Kareste's face. That hurt him, even though he knew it was not her. Suddenly, he realized that he could hear that same hiss in the tops of the trees all around them, and then he understood that all the while that she had been talking her voice was also reflected in the wood. The sound of it was in the hollows of tree trunks, in the whispering of leaves, in the slow creak and mutter of tree roots. It was in the bubbling of water in a rill somewhere further into the wood and out of sight, and it was even in the slow seeping of water though the earth.

He understood now what had troubled him all along about her voice, for there was power in it, and all the while that she spoke it was gathering itself, building, forming some spell, and only at the last did his instincts perceive it. At the last, and perhaps too late.

There was a sudden noise. It was shrill. From all around them it came, and Brand understood even as it drove into his ears, turning, twisting, piercing like a hot needle, what it was. All the sound for miles had been turned into a weapon by the witch. Her magic had taken it, transformed it, compressed it into a single thing and sent it tunnelling into their ears. It was unbearable.

Kareste fell off her horse, yet she managed to hold onto Shurilgar's staff. Brand could not think. He was dizzy, and the pain drove him like a madness. He wanted to act, to do something to relieve it, but it only grew and scattered his thoughts to the wind.

All the while he heard the voice of the witch beyond the shrill sound that speared into him. She chanted, and though he did not understand the words, he perceived that her power was growing as the need for subterfuge was gone. Soon, she would kill them.

Brand struggled to control his mount. The idea came to him to ride the witch down, but he floundered in a sea of pain and confusion. It took him some moments to realize that the horse's reins were no longer in his hand but had fallen and trailed between its legs.

Durletha's chanting rose to a higher pitch. If it were possible, the pain redoubled. Brand's vision swam, and he knew that there were only moments left before he fell from the horse as had Kareste.

And then he heard another sound. Faint at first, but something different from the high-pitched daggers in his ears. It was Bragga Mor's flute. As it had been earlier, so was it now: beautiful, sweet, haunting.

The chanting of the witch faltered for just a moment. She seemed perplexed by how to take this new sound up into her attack. In that moment Kareste regained her feet. She staggered up, but she did not attack with her sword or try to summon power from Shurilgar's staff.

Brand, his newfound senses growing day by day, dimly perceived her mind reach out, and her own power become one with the music of the flute.

He was staggered by the shadowy sense of what she was doing. With skill and precision her power became one with the music, and swift as thought took hold of it and transformed it into a kind of shield. It veiled them from the witch's attack, not nullifying it completely, but subduing it so that it was no more than an unpleasant noise.

He realized that though his sensitivity to lòhrengai was growing, he had only the same skill in the craft as a young boy picking up a sword for the first time. It had taken him years of hard practice to acquire the skill to be bodyguard to the king, and that same effort awaited him if ever he wished to become proficient with the power that was in him.

He shut down that line of thinking. It was yet another way the magic inside him tempted him to its use, for to learn a skill was a challenge, and the harder something was to achieve the more Brand set his mind to attain it.

All sound in the wood now seemed muffled, yet still Brand heard the witch shriek. Whether it was in anger or pain, he did not know, but he sensed her frustration and knew instinctively that the danger had not passed. She would not give up on claiming the staff, and a new attack was imminent.

As soon as Brand had that thought he knew that he must attack to forestall her. But driven by need rather than considered reason, his body reacted with an instinct of its own, or at least the magic that was in him did.

Without thinking he raised Aranloth's staff. Fire burst from it; a hot wild stream that roared to life and leaped at the witch like a living thing.

He rode toward her, forgetting his sword and concentrating only on the flame.

Kareste moved also. No flame came from Shurilgar's staff, but it was raised in threat. It was a threat that Durletha saw and understood. She understood also that her attack had failed. Temptation had not worked, nor surprise. And she did not like it.

The witch hissed again. Her left arm she held up as a shield, and by the power that was in her she rebuffed Brand's flame. A small thing for her to do, and easily could she turn it aside and launch her own assault upon him. But for this Kareste waited, for in that moment she would strike herself, and the witch would be open to a greater attack, directed by skill and strength.

"Begone!" Kareste yelled, taking up Brand's words.

The witch looked at them, poised amid the flame, beaten, but not defeated.

"This is not over," she said. "It will never be over until that staff is in my hands, and then the other half after it. Old as the hills I am, and I have patience. I'll watch you fall yet, and it will be all the sweeter."

With a toss of her ash-blond hair she fixed Brand with a look of hatred, and he wished never to see such a look again, for it was Kareste, Kareste as she would be if she fell to the Shadow and refused to destroy the staff at the end. It was the way she would look at him if they fought, and fight they must, no matter that it was the last thing he wanted, if that came to pass. For he saw now more clearly than ever before, understood so much better Aranloth's warning, that for the sake of Alithoras the staff must be destroyed. Otherwise, the evil in the world would constantly seek it.

One moment the witch was before them, her ash-blond hair tossing, and then she was gone. In her place were the flicking wings of a hawk and a fierce cry from its hooked beak. The pale underwings flashed. Feathers beat the air and swift as an arrow it drove, talons outstretched, at Brand's face.

He ducked, but not quick enough. Talons ripped and clawed, seeking for his eyes, yet his head was now bent low and the shrieking attack struck only the helm of the Duthenor.

There was a flash of silver light, and then the hawk shot upward into the air and was gone.

Brand and Kareste looked at each other. They did not speak. The only sound they heard was the playing of the flute.

They turned to Bragga Mor. Tears ran down his face, and the music, up close as they were to it now, filled them with sadness and a sense of longing for something forever beyond reach. It had saved them, but it was heartbreaking, and Brand felt the outside edges of a sorrow greater than any he had ever known. It was a grief that this stranger endured every day.

Bragga Mor ceased playing, and he looked at them with eyes sadder even than the music.

8. What Hope for Cardoroth?

Aranloth stood still. His hands were raised, and only the sleeves of his robe moved, fluttering in the northerly breeze. Gilhain felt the same air on his face.

For a moment, the stench of the serpent was gone. The air was sweet once more, sweeping down from the north, from the mountains that Gilhain had never seen nor now ever would. He even fancied that he smelled the scent of pinewoods and snow – crisp and fresh.

He heard a grinding noise and more stone popped to dust under the enormous pressure exerted by the serpent's tightening coils. The odor of stone overpowered whatever else Gilhain smelled, for it was driven into his face by the north wind which gusted stronger, moment by moment.

With the wind came cold. Either that, or the shadow of death that fell over the wall blotted out all warmth and drained the air of life.

The wind now blew with genuine force, whistling through the crenels and moaning along the sides of the merlons. All the while, the lòhrens stood unmoving.

Gilhain felt something on his cheek. At first, he thought it was crumbled stone from the battlement, and then he knew that it was sleet.

The wind suddenly died. Yet it remained cold, strangely cold given how hot it was before. So cold that Gilhain noticed with amazement that white frost began to settle in patches over the stonework of the Cardurleth.

He looked about him. The soldiers were shivering, and a great shudder ran through his own body. He looked at the blade of his sword. It glittered with ice.

Gilhain whipped his head around in astonishment. Even the serpent was coated by a layer of rime: the slime that dripped from its belly was now turned to a dirty white crust.

And the serpent did nothing to shake off its icy coat. It lay, twisted and sluggish, over the Cardurleth. The coils no longer tightened. The dust of crumbled stone no longer filled the air.

Nothing moved in the icy stillness, not until a sudden sign from Lornach to a few of the Durlin. They leaped across the rampart and closed the short distance between themselves and the serpent in the flicker of an eye. They hacked with their swords, but these were still useless. Then Lornach seized a long spear from a nearby soldier, and Taingern joined him.

Together the two men positioned the spear beneath the creature's pale belly. And then they drove it upward with slow precision. The air from their lungs billowed out in a silvery mist about them, and the spear, driven with their combined strength, guided by four hands, penetrated the thick skin.

The serpent moved with a spasm. Cold or no, sluggish or not, it felt pain for the first time and lifted its body away from it.

A great coil rose. The belly shone pale beneath. Blood dripped from the spear wound, turning to dark ice as it spattered the stone.

The two men did not relent. They followed the creature, continuing to push the spear upward by clambering atop the merlons.

With another great heave the coil lifted high above them. The spear was taken beyond their reach, and they tumbled from the merlons back onto the rampart. The coil rose higher, the spear sticking from it, and then with a twist and thrash the loop of the serpent's body dropped once more.

More merlons burst. Men were crushed. The two Durlin scrabbled away from the rubble, and the serpent shuddered, raising up the coil with a jerk more sudden than the first, for its efforts had only driven the spear deep; the full six foot length of it now pierced the creature.

It thrashed. Coils rose and fell all along the Cardurleth. For a moment it hung there, roiling in pain, but then the extremity of its anguish drove it to twist too far. With a final undulation of its whole body, it lost its grip on the battlement and fell.

Down the massive creature plummeted. It thrashed as it went, and when it landed it sent a tremor through the earth and the battlement shook. There in the dust it writhed. A long time it would take to die, but Gilhain had no doubt that it would. Somehow, Cardoroth was saved.

On unsteady legs the king walked over and looked down. The creature churned violently in its death pangs. Blood streamed from its wound. He looked along the battlement. The men were in shock, but quickly they began to clean the rampart of bodies and broken stone. The lòhrens all along the Cardurleth leaned on their staffs.

He turned toward Aranloth, but did not see him at first. Then, some way from the broken edge of the rampart, he spotted him, collapsed to the ground.

He raced over. From afar he heard the groaning of the enemy horde, and also the pain-filled screech of elùgroths. When he came to Aranloth the old man's eyes flickered open, and the lòhren spoke, his voice soft but grim.

"Thus do they pay for their sorcery," he said. "They linked themselves to the serpent to bring it here and keep it in this world. And as it dies, so too do the weakest among them."

Aranloth spoke no more. His eyes blinked strangely, and then closed. Gilhain looked at him, dread creeping though his veins even though he had thought that after the serpent nothing could scare him again. But dread was worse than fear – dread spoke of human tragedy and loss that was irrevocable, but yet to come.

The king bent down and felt for a pulse. He could not find one, but he had little skill with such matters. The Durlin had more.

He looked up to call one over, but Taingern was already striding toward him. The Durlin kneeled. With deft movements he felt at Aranloth's wrist and neck.

Gilhain knew that he should have seen this coming. The lòhrens had no prop as did the elùgroths. For them, there was no artifact such as Shurilgar's staff. What they did, they did by the power that was in them, and by the strength of their will and the courage of their hearts. And Aranloth, oldest and greatest among them, he who had given most for the longest, had perhaps finally given too much.

Gilhain felt suddenly cold.

"Well?" he asked.

Taingern did not look at him, did not remove his intent gaze from the lòhren.

"I don't know. I thought I felt a pulse, but then it was gone. Sometimes, it's hard to find."

Gilhain did not quite believe that. The Durlin had some skill in healing. It was necessary, for they might have to help someone before a proper healer could arrive. There were times when battlefield medicine, the treatments given to a wounded man while the blood spurted from him, later made the difference between life and death. At other times, if not done correctly, the man was dead before help arrived at all.

59

Gilhain bit his lip. Yet, he saw that Taingern had not stopped feeling for a pulse, and that surely must be a good thing.

The king remained where he was. He took the lòhren's hand, the hand of his old friend. But beyond friendship there was this also – the fate of the city was bound to him. Without Aranloth to lead them, the other lòhrens were no match for the elùgroths. What hope for Cardoroth without him?

9. The Shadow is Rising

The sad music of Bragga Mor trailed away.

"Who *are* you?" Kareste asked.

"I'm a bard," he replied, "A wanderer. A man without a home."

Brand felt sorry for him. He guessed his origin, and if he was right, there was reason for the man's sadness. He sensed also that he had no wish to talk about it.

"Where will you go now?" he asked. "You've made an enemy of the witch."

"She would not be the first. Yet, in this case, I'm in no danger. It's the staff she wants, and if the stories I know about it are true, I can see why. She will follow you and not me. Though I would not care to cross paths with her in the future." The man sighed. "I'll continue to wander, going wherever my horse takes me."

They did not spend long with Bragga Mor. He invited them to eat with him, and they did, enjoying the roasted hare. In return, they gave him some small supply of dried fruit and nuts. Their own provisions were getting low, and Brand knew that soon he must begin to hunt or forage. That would not be easy, and worse, it would take time. And time was something they had little of.

"Know this," Bragga Mor said when they parted. "The Shadow is rising, but ever men contend with it. Even as it is here, so too is it in other places. It never conquers unopposed."

With those words he mounted his steed and rode slowly away. Brand did not think they would meet again, which was a pity: he liked him. Yet the ways of fate and fortune were mysterious, and he sensed, for no reason that he could see at all, but with confident certainty nonetheless, that Bragga Mor had a vital part to play in the future of Alithoras.

"What chance brought him to us?" Kareste asked.

"Who knows, but it was a good chance, if chance it was."

They mounted and rode out of the wood. There was no sign of Durletha, but she would be about somewhere. She would attack them again, Brand knew. Or, more disturbingly, she would set a trap for them. He must be on his guard.

They kept the river close by on their right as they travelled. Day by day it kept them company, for its constant gurgle and splash was like a familiar companion. But they did not approach it too closely. Its banks were lined by trees, and Brand preferred to stay in the open where no ambush could be set.

The weather was good; the grass was green and the sky a brilliant blue. Each day was such a day as made Brand glad to be alive, for Alithoras was a beautiful land and he could never see too much of it.

Where they travelled now was much like his homeland, only here it was empty of people, and the lack of ploughed fields and livestock seemed peculiar. But there was no lack of wildlife, and some of it was strange to him. But he heard often the familiar sounds of *nudaluk* birds, and hares and foxes were everywhere. He saw no deer though, but feed was plentiful at the moment. In winter, they would be drawn closer to the better pastures on the river flats.

They stopped to camp one evening as dusk fell. It crept over the land, and it brought peace with it, as it always did. This was Brand's favorite time of day, and there were few things better than working hard through the daylight hours, and then laying down tools of an evening to enjoy the peace and quiet and to contemplate the day's achievements. But that was a farmer's life, not a warrior's, and he saw no way that he would ever obtain those simple pleasures that he longed for again.

They set up their camp with practiced efficiency, each performing tasks by established routine, and then they sat down and talked.

Brand enjoyed these fireside conversations with her. During the day they were always in haste and their minds were on finding a safe path forward. Also, she only seemed to truly come alive in the evening. She was not a morning person as was he, and she seemed to respond to starlight and night better than sun and blue skies.

Smoke curled lazily upward, soon lost in the dark heavens. The burning timber shimmered with warmth. Coals formed, red-hot gledes that glimmered like precious jewels. There was a pop, and then a spray of sparks, and he realized, quite suddenly, quite unexpectedly, that he was smitten by her. No sparkle of any jewel was as precious to him as a fleeting glance from her eyes.

The realization took his breath away. He could imagine the rest of his life with her. It was not hard to do so. But with a sinking feeling he understood also that she had no such desire. She was caught up in her own troubles at the moment, always deep in thought and of divided mind. She felt for the Halathrin entrapped by sorcery, and a part of her wanted to fight to free them. But another part was lured by the power in Shurilgar's staff. And how much of the former was a dissimilitude of the latter, either her own or of the power in the staff?

He did not know which part of her was the strongest. And there was a darkness in her past, too. She had never openly said as much, but she sought power not just for the sake of it, not just to protect herself, but to take revenge on elugs. Elugs had killed her family and destroyed the life she once knew. And Shurilgar's staff offered a means to wreak dreadful havoc upon them. She had no time for him, and she might yet fall to the Shadow. If that happened she would be lost to him forever, and he felt suddenly cold to the marrow of his bones. But he must give her the freedom to choose, for without temptation there was no certainty of choice. Only the first made the second real.

The smoke curled into the starry night, otherworldly and elusive. All his hopes rode on the whims of a fate that he could not see, just as invisible currents of air took the smoke.

He hoped the king could forgive him, if he was even still alive. But life was one risk after another, one choice piled on top of endless decisions, and if he risked Cardoroth he did so for good reason. Khamdar was right: Kareste had it in her to be great. If she turned to the Light, she could give Alithoras hope. At least, he wished so, just as he hoped that those he respected most in the world would see things the way he saw them. But he was no longer sure if his judgement was sound. Emotion clouded it.

He looked at Kareste and found that she was looking at him.

"Are we doing the right thing?" he asked. "Have I the right to jeopardize a whole city?"

Kareste seemed taken aback by the question. "I don't know," she said at length. "Who is to say what's right or wrong? But I know this much at least – I'm most wary of anyone who *does* have all the answers."

Brand suddenly grinned. "You're dead right there."

The fire popped and cracked. Kareste looked at him, one side of her face lit up by the flames, the other in shadow.

"Why so philosophical?" she asked.

"Aren't I always?" he replied.

She raised an eyebrow. "Actually, most men claim to be, at least when they're talking to girls, but few are. You're one of the few."

He gave a little bow from where he sat, but did not answer.

"So," she said. "While you're in this mood, what's the meaning of life?"

It was his turn to be taken aback. "You might be better off asking Aranloth that. He's lived more of it than I have."

"True. Maybe I *will* ask him one day, but just now I'm asking you."

He looked into the fire. It was dying down to embers. It would not last, and suddenly it occurred to him that nothing ever did. His time with Kareste would come to an end one day, just as this conversation would. The only difference was the time it took. But time was a strange thing. The past was hazy, the future clouded. The only time that counted was the here and now. It was a somewhat depressing thought, and then he thought that even depression and joy were transient.

He smiled sadly. "I don't know the meaning of life. I'm not sure that there *is* one – unless we choose one for ourselves."

"And what have you chosen?"

"To give rather than to take. To enjoy a cold drink after a hard day's work. To follow it with a fine meal, preferably cooked with food I've grown myself. And to see the flashing smile of a girl I like. Most of all, to be kind. There's not enough kindness in the world."

She looked at him a long time. "Many would call that simplistic."

"I'm a simple man."

She grinned at him suddenly. "Then you've fooled me."

"What do *you* think?" he asked. "What's the meaning of life?"

She looked away. "I don't know, but I'll think on what you've said."

10. If only Chance Allowed...

The seconds slipped by. Each one seemed to Gilhain as an hour, but at length Taingern paused in his search for a pulse. The Durlin held two fingers steadily against Aranloth's throat.

"Well?" the king asked.

"There's a heartbeat," Taingern replied. "It's weak, but it's there."

Relief washed through Gilhain, but he shut it down. Whatever ailed Aranloth was so serious as to bring him near to death. And he might still die without proper help. This was no time for emotion, but one for action.

He stood and strode to the nearest soldier. "Quickly!" he said. "Go and fetch the healer Arell. Make sure it's her – not any other will do."

The soldier saluted and ran off.

The king moved back to Aranloth. The Durlin had appropriated a stretcher – there were many being brought up to the wall now to take the dead or injured back into the city. They had laid Aranloth upon it.

"Good," the king said. "But we'll wait here. I've sent for Arell, and she'll know where to find us. I won't trust him to the other healers."

He did not wait for a reply. Quickly, he signaled another soldier over.

"Go to the stone mason's guild. They have their headquarters near the palace. Do you know the building?"

"Yes, my Lord."

"Tell whoever's there that I want their three best experts to meet me here. And I want them as soon as possible. We must make repairs to the wall. Run!"

The soldier did not salute but sprinted away.

Gilhain turned to yet another soldier. "You," he said. "Get me a lòhren."

The soldier glanced at where Aranloth lay on the stretcher.

"Right away, sir."

It was not long before Arell came. She moved without seeming haste, yet her eyes took everything in at a glance and in a moment she knelt beside the lòhren and examined him.

She took the lòhren's pulse at the wrist as had Taingern, only she seemed to take three at slightly different locations. She then took the throat pulse in the same place as had Taingern, but she surprised Gilhain when she removed one of Aranloth's boots and took a pulse at his foot.

She did not give any indication of her thoughts, and Gilhain did not interrupt her. For a moment she pressed her palm over the lòhren's chest, though what she was doing was hard to guess. Then she placed her fingers on his earlobe and gave a sharp squeeze. Aranloth seemed to shrink away from the pain, but he raised no hand to try to brush away the cause. If this worried her she gave no sign, unless it was a slight frown that had not been there before.

She checked his eyes next, tilting his head back and forth to let in more or less light.

During the course of her examination another lòhren arrived. This was a seemingly young man, though it was hard to tell with lòhrens. He wore the same white robes as them all, but his hair was shoulder length and blond. What his nationality was Gilhain could not guess, but he was calm, even after seeing his master lying unconscious on a stretcher.

Arell finished her examination and stood. She spoke to the king, but her gaze strayed to the lòhren.

"He's near to death," she said. "Very near, though I can find no injuries. He may have had a stroke, but the signs in his pulses don't indicate that. My king, I don't know what ails him."

Gilhain thought about that. Healers never admitted that they did not know what was wrong. It was, he thought, her way of saying that not only did she not know what was wrong, but that she knew of no treatment to keep him alive. That was something that must be faced, and given the state of the siege, she knew he must prepare for it.

She looked at the young lòhren. "I don't know of any medical cause for his collapse, but perhaps it has more to do with magic?"

The lòhren gave a slight nod. "If it helps, I can tell you this much. Likely, he expended too much power and exhausted himself. To use lòhrengai takes a great mental effort – it's hard like physical work. And just as a man can work too hard and collapse, so it is with lòhrengai. He has taxed his mind beyond its endurance. Worse, he does not have his staff, which grounds his mind to this world. Now, it may roam other worlds, or other realms beside the physical. It is caught out of time, neither here, nor really anywhere else, though I cannot be sure of the latter."

"And how do lòhrens treat this?"

The young man shook his head. "There's no treatment. We're taught never to let it happen in the first place, unless we're prepared to die. I've never seen this before, but I've heard of it. He might live, or he might die. There's nothing to be done." He paused, showing the first sign of nerves. "I wish there were…"

Arell thought for some moments before she addressed Gilhain again.

"I may be able to keep him alive for a while, at least his body. That may give his spirit, if you believe in such things, time to return."

The young lòhren shook his head. "Without his spirit, the body will wither and die swiftly. At least, so our lore of such things says. Aranloth would know more…"

There was a pause. The king eventually forced himself to ask the question that he did not wish to ask.

"So nothing can be done to save him?"

Arell did not speak. Nor the young lòhren. They had no answers. In truth, Gilhain knew, not all questions had an answer. It was a bitter truth of life.

He dismissed the lòhren, who walked slowly back toward his white-robed comrades. There was no one left but him and Arell.

"Take him to the palace," Gilhain said. "In you I trust, for once you brought me back from the dead. But I'll tell you the truth now. I don't expect any miracles from you – I know you'll do everything you can. If he dies, it won't be through a lack of your trying. But know this: if he *does* die, Cardoroth is unprotected. The elùgroths will be too strong for us."

Arell looked him straight in the eye. "Can we not hold against the enemy?"

Gilhain returned her gaze. "You told me the truth about Aranloth before. Now, I'll tell you the truth about our situation. We cannot hold for long against either the elùgroths or the horde. The rumors that you have heard are true. We sent Brand on a quest. It's the one true hope for Cardoroth. If he fails, we will fall, sooner or later. But know this, the elùgroth lied. Brand is not dead; at least we don't think so. And hope for Cardoroth lives so long as he does."

Surprisingly, Arell laughed. "I never believed Brand was dead. Many in the city do, but not me. I *know* him. He's hard to kill. If anyone can find a way to succeed in whatever task you set him, it's him."

She called for some soldiers and got them to lift up Aranloth's stretcher. Quickly she gave them instructions on where to go, and she followed after them, a thoughtful but determined expression on her face.

Aurellin came to the king's side. "Will he live?" she asked, straight to the point as she usually was.

Gilhain bowed his head. He made no attempt to hide his feelings from her.

"No," he answered. "Arell will do what she can, but she cannot do the impossible. Neither she nor the young lòhren offered any hope. Aranloth gave too deeply of his power to save us, and he will now pay the price, as he must have known he would."

Aurellin put her arm around him. "Aranloth seldom got the respect he deserved. Always he put his life at risk for others. And if the legends are true, he's been doing that for many lives of men. I've often wondered what drives him, for surely something in his past must do so."

Her gaze followed the departing healer, and then she shook her head. "But it's too early to speak yet of death. Once, Arell saved your own life, and there was then less hope than there is now for the lòhren."

"That's true. But she had Brand with her then. Now, she's alone."

"Perhaps," Aurellin said. "But then again, it was not Brand who effected your cure. She did that herself, and Brand merely saved her from the same assassin that tried to kill you."

He smiled sadly. "Ever the optimist, aren't you?"

"There's no other way to live. Though I suppose some try."

"Well, if you still have hope, then so do I."

She took his hand. "Hope is good, but it can be cheated too. From the moment Brand and Arell met, I thought they were meant for each other. But nothing ever came of it."

Gilhain grinned for just a moment. "Maybe not. But then again he reached out to her and had her teach the Durlin basic healing skills. They've spent much time together, though most of it was hidden away in the Durlin chapterhouse."

"That, I didn't know. Well, perhaps there's hope for them after all."

"Brand has wandering feet though," he said. "There's something in him that wants to explore, to go where he's never been before. I'm not sure if he'll ever settle down."

She pursed her lips. "Maybe. But I don't believe it for a second. He wants to see the land as you said, but he wants more to settle down with a girl. He'd put aside his sword, his fame, all his training and ambition; he'd put aside everything to start a farm – and a family, if only chance allowed…"

Gilhain scratched his chin. "You mean if I set him free of my service."

"That too."

"And what of the Duthenor? Do you think, now that he's grown into a man, that he'll leave the usurper to continue ruling his people unchallenged?"

Her eyes narrowed. "No. You're right there." She paused. "But I see better why nothing has happened yet between him and Arell. I was sure it would, but if so, he would not leave her here while he went home. Nor would he lead her into danger. That explains much, very much indeed. But freeing the Duthenor from tyranny is one thing; ruling them himself is another. He might attempt the first, and if successful, forgo the second. In fact, I think he would. He has no wish to rule others."

"A very interesting observation," Gilhain said thoughtfully. "One that I've also made myself."

Aurellin looked at him sharply. Likely enough, she knew exactly what he was thinking. She usually did.

11. Magic, not Medicine

Arell had time to think as she followed the stretcher-bearers toward the palace. In the distance, the elug war drums began to rumble to slow life once more. She was sick of them. She was sick of many things, but she endured. And endurance had always served her well.

Her beginnings were humble. Her prospects had been poor. And she was too strong willed, too ambitious, to merely use her looks to attract a husband of wealth. Not that she disdained the girls she grew up with who used wiles to attract a partner of influence. The idea had occurred to her too, but something else drove her. She had a thirst for knowledge, and marriage and children would not satisfy her. Not completely, anyway.

That thirst for knowledge took a special form – a desire to understand the human body, to cure illness, to slow aging, to make people's lives better. It was a worthy goal. But a goal, at least in Cardoroth, reserved as the special province of men.

She learned and studied under bearded old healers, never more than a servant to them, never having any real hope of being more than their pretty flunky. But she kept her mouth shut and her eyes open – and learned – and endured. Until one day Brand exposed her master as a fraud and propelled her into the light. For she had learned her lessons well through long years of servitude, and he had given her the chance to save the king's life.

It was a kingly gift, for Brand had earned enemies that day. The bearded old man knew other bearded old men, and they talked and plotted and schemed against him. But he was Brand, and he smiled at them when he saw them, but he did not turn his back on them.

Now, she wore the white smock of a healer herself, the only female in Cardoroth to do so. Though many still called her a witch behind her back, even those who begged her to heal them when they were sick, she had prosperity and fame. But not respect. Then again, the king respected her, and the queen, and the Durlin. And there was always Brand. There was *always* him. The esteem of a few like that was worth more than the veneration of the masses.

She followed the stretcher-bearers to the palace and the chambers of healing situated within its east wing. These rooms were shared by several healers, those old men she despised so much, but medications and equipment were close to hand.

The rooms could be noisy, for the king paid the healers to see not just to palace staff but every morning and every evening they opened the doors to the poor. And the poor were many, and often in need of treatment.

Barok was there, though he was not busy. He paid her little attention though, until he saw who was on the stretcher. His eyes widened at that, and she could see his mind working and knew where it would take him.

She went into a room. It was empty, containing little more than a bed. What she wished most for was a door though, but there were none anywhere in the chambers of healing. Had there been one, she would have closed and barred it.

Barok followed her inside, as she knew he would. He was in charge of these rooms, and the only healer left because all others now served in rooms close to the Cardurleth. He was going to try to take over, for to heal Aranloth would win him praise, and praise meant fame and money.

"Gently," she instructed the soldiers as they began to transfer the lòhren from the stretcher to the bed.

"You've done well to bring him here," Barok said.

She raised an eyebrow and shot him a flinty look with the other eye. It was no easy thing to do, and it usually had the desired effect. But Barok had seen an opportunity and he would not be so easily put off.

He ignored her and made ready to commence an examination.

"Out!" Arell said with intense force, but still quietly. "I didn't bring him here so that you could squint at him and pretend you had an idea of what was going on. Out!"

Barok turned. He gave her his own look. It was one of superiority. His pale hands, nearly as white as the smock he wore, were clasped in front of him. He peered down at her, eyes cold as they studied her from above his long beard. It was a look that she had seen him use on troublesome patients, but it had no effect on her.

"Out!" she repeated.

"Don't you think someone of Aranloth's stature deserves treatment from one of Cardoroth's finest healers?" He looked at her, leaving no doubt in his expression that he did not consider her worthy of the task.

Arell had had enough. "The king placed him in my care, and I'll do what can be done." She spoke quietly, her voice filled with icy determination, and it carried an edge of threat. "Speak with the king – if you dare interrupt him while the city teeters on the edge of destruction. If he places Aranloth in your care, so be it. But while we argue, the lòhren's life slips away. Now stand aside, for I'll not tolerate any further delay. Don't interrupt me again except at the king's word."

She made to move past him, but Barok blocked her path.

"I'm in charge here. I'll treat the lòhren. I don't know what the king said, but there are ways of making such pronouncements officially, and I've seen no paperwork nor heard from any messenger. *You* can go and get leave from the king to treat the lòhren. Until then, I'll do what needs doing."

Arell wanted to slap him, but that would not be enough. He was too thick headed for that to work, and time was running out. Instead, she made one swift move and drew a knife from her boot.

The blade gleamed wickedly between them, and she would use it if she had to. If Aranloth died, the city would fall.

Barok looked at her in astonishment, but what he was going to say, she would never know.

Taingern strode past her and before Barok even realized what was happening the Durlin had grabbed him in a headlock and manhandled him out the door. When they were in the corridor, he threw him to the floor.

"Fool!" he said. "That's your message from the king. "And if you step inside this room again, I'll kill you. Cardoroth needs the lòhren, but it doesn't need *you*."

The Durlin drew his sword to emphasize the point.

Barok scrambled to his feet. This was more than he expected, more even than Arell expected; but it proved the point that Cardoroth was on the edge.

The healer fled, and his dignity went with him, but Arell was already moving to Aranloth as the sound of Barok's retreat pounded away into the distance. Faintly, she heard him yell when he reached somewhere he considered safe: *this is beyond her – the lòhren will die, or worse, she'll kill him with ineptitude.*

She spared Taingern a brief look of thanks as she sheathed her knife.

"Pay him no heed," the Durlin said. "Not for nothing are you the king's own healer. Not for nothing did Brand recruit you to train the Durlin. And not for nothing does Brand speak highly of you."

She gave a little bow. "May I prove your confidence in me."

Once more she examined the lòhren. He was no better, and she knew with the certainty of natural instinct and honed skill combined that no art of medicine could bring him back. They needed magic for that, but it seemed not even the lòhrens themselves could achieve such a thing. If it was possible, perhaps only the greatest lòhren of them all knew how, but he lay silent and dying on the bed before her.

She sat and thought. There were medicines that might make his heart beat faster, for it was slow now, so slow as to be pumping blood at half the rate that it should. No wonder that his pulse was hard to take. But those medicines were no cure. They would buy some time, but time for what?

Taingern sat near her. He did not speak, did not ask questions that would interrupt her flow of thought. She appreciated that. He was a thoughtful and kind man, notwithstanding his earlier violence.

But the more she thought the deeper she sunk in a pool of despair. It swallowed her up, drowned her in hopelessness. It was not enough to prolong Aranloth's life for a day or two. It was not *enough*!

She stood and looked out the window. The city stretched out before her. Her city, and it would fall. Of that, there was no doubt.

Brand was out there beyond it, somewhere in the vast land of Alithoras. He gave her hope. They must endure; they must survive the enemy for as long as they could to give him the time to do what he must do. And only

Aranloth had the power to stem the dark tide of sorcery the elùgroths would throw against them. The other lòhrens would fight, and they would die. Against the might of the enemy they would not stand long without their leader.

She must *think*. Medicine was of no avail. Perhaps magic would help, but there was no magic in the city except for the lòhrens, and they had admitted they knew of no way to bring Aranloth's spirit back to his body. But if magic had freed it from the bonds of the flesh, then magic could summon it back. That was only logical. But if not the magic of the lòhrens, then whose?

There were witches in Cardoroth. But they had no real magic, at least so she believed. Their talent lay more in foresight and prophecy. It was too far to go to Lòrenta for more help; Aranloth would be dead before such a journey even began, not to mention that an army barred the way, and the lòhrens left in Lòrenta probably knew no more than the ones here.

Barok's words haunted her. This was beyond her skill. Aranloth *would* die. It made her feel no better that he would die no matter who cared for him. The other healers would fuss and meddle. They would draw blood and prescribe herbs and potions. None of it would work.

She had done what could be done. It was a simple thing. She had positioned him on pillows so that he half sat in the bed. That allowed him to breathe a little better. Soon, she might give him a medicine that would make his heart beat faster. But that put strain on it also, and it came with risks. There was nothing else to be done, and she must face defeat.

She looked through the glass window. They were on a lower floor of the palace, but they still had a good view. There were many houses out there. All along the streets were homes where she had healed people. They were everywhere, all the way to the Tower of Halathgar and beyond.

Her mind wandered, and then it focused on the tower. It was distant, but it stood tall and strange. It was a great landmark in the city, the tower of the Witch Queen. The tower of Carnhaina, who had once ruled in Cardoroth. *She* had power. Power beyond an ordinary lòhren. Power enough to rival Aranloth himself. And there were stories of what the queen had done with that power. Arell had read of them in medical textbooks.

That gave her pause for thought. Carnhaina was a battle queen, not a healer. And yet there was a story of some healing that she had done. A distinct image of the book's cover came to Arell, and fragments of the story with it.

She bit her lip and looked at Taingern. There was another story, a story that Brand himself had told her of Carnhaina, though she was long dead and become dust.

"The Forgotten Queen," she whispered. "Carnhaina."

That was all she said, but Taingern's face paled. She read fear in his expression, or perhaps awe, and it was confirmation that Brand's story was true; not that she doubted him, but it was a wild story, a story to frighten even brave men. It was also a story that just now gave her hope. And even if it was a wild hope, desperate and no doubt dangerous, it was still *hope*.

"Let no one into the room!" she said.

She raced away. The corridors were empty, though there were patients in some of the rooms. She saw no sign of Barok, and it was just as well for him. The knife was still in her boot, and she would use it if he got in her way.

She sped up a flight of stairs, taking them two at a time, and then spun around a corner and flung open a door.

Inside was the library of the healers. She knew each book, though there were hundreds. She had read them all, studied them, committed their knowledge to her memory. Much was false, proven wrong by her own experiments, but much was true and valuable.

She headed straight for the book she sought. It was old. Its cover was black, faded to gray. Gold script covered it, and the sign of Halathgar was there as well, the constellation that the Forgotten Queen had taken for her seal.

Arell raced back. She had an idea, but the book would give her the confirmation that she needed. But even if her memory was correct, the look on Taingern's face when she mentioned Carnhaina gave her pause for thought. And, given the story Brand had told her, well it might.

12. Blood Calls to Blood

Arell returned to the room. Even in so little time the fear that Aranloth had already died near paralyzed her.

She stopped running when she neared the entrance. Haste was not a good look for a healer; it inspired a sense of panic, and that was not what patients, or anybody else, ever needed.

She methodically checked the lòhren's pulse again when she returned, and she hid her relief that he still lived as much as she hid her fear that he had died.

"What've you got there?" Taingern asked, gesturing at the book.

"It's old," she replied. "It must have been copied several times, for the language, while stilted, is modern."

She sat down and opened it. For one brief moment she looked at him, noted that his face still seemed pale, and then she put her head down and flicked through the pages.

"It was written in the court of Queen Carnhaina. The author, one Karappe, was a great healer, responsible for many of the treatises that we still use today – but this is more a memoire of his queen's accomplishments."

"That's not a Camar name."

"No. He was a foreigner. "The queen rescued him from a battlefield somewhere when he was a child. He thought of her as a mother, and in a strange kind of way that was exactly what she was to him."

She paused, flicking carefully through the pages. The earlier parts dealt with Carnhaina's ascension to the throne, and then her first battles. She skipped those chapters, seeking one of the last ones where the queen was

82

old. Old, of course, was a relative term. The events in the book had occurred near on a thousand years ago.

She nearly held her breath when she found the chapter that she wanted.

"This is it. It's a little story, one of many the healer tells about Carnhaina. But all his stories serve a purpose."

She paused, and then began to read out a sentence here or there to give Taingern the gist of events.

So it came to pass that the lòhren Gavnor, the least of the lòhrens in Queen Carnhaina's court, attempted to Spirit Walk.

She read on, swiftly passing by much else that was interesting.

At length, the bonds of the flesh were broken; his spirit soared. He saw what was, and what yet may be, and he reported to his queen … but the enemy discovered him. Thus was he assailed. Pursued by those of greater might, he fled. Chased incessantly, he retreated into the uttermost darkness. There, he lost his enemies. They dared not follow. Yet, in saving himself, he therefore was lost also. Too far he strayed. Too weak was become the link between body and spirit. On the brink his life hovered…

Arell read on. It was clear to her that the healer was reporting things that he did not fully understand, yet it was the essence of his story that counted, not the details.

Gavnor was a favorite of the queen. She desired his service, and not even death would she let prevent it. At great risk to herself…

"Some of this just doesn't make sense," Arell said.

Blood calls to blood she proclaimed. And Gavnor was related to her through her father's line … Her face was set. No doubt she showed. With a swift motion she cut herself. The small blade, marked with the Sign of Halathgar, cut with ease. Sharp it was. Her palm seemed uninjured, and then her royal blood sprang forth. She that was queen bled like a commoner, but no common act it was: rather it was a deed of nobility … Red her blood was, and bright, and her Court muttered in astonishment and averted their gazes. She laughed at them, her deep-throated laugh filled with disdain and courage and defiance. She that was as a Queen of the World cared nothing for their petty opinions. Gavnor was of her blood, and she would save him if it could be done.

"There is more like that. Karappe cared little for her court, it seems, though his love of her is plain.

Queen Carnhaina spoke, her voice haughty and prideful as ever. To Gavnor she called, her great utterances ringing through the uttermost dark … And Gavnor, hearing and obeying, came back into the light. Thus did the queen recall her servant; thus did blood call to blood.

"There's more, but that's all that counts."

Taingern looked at her stonily. He knew what she intended, and he did not like it. Yet he did not try to talk her out of it.

"Speak, Taingern. Am I mad, or is there some hope, however slim, in this?"

He sighed. "As Brand obviously told you, we met her once. Her spirit at least. We saved her tomb from a sorcerer. Of that, I'll not speak. But to try to summon her, to summon her by asking the king to spill his own blood, well, that is doubly bold."

"But do you think it'll work? I have here the very words that Carnhaina spoke, and Gilhain is of her line. Blood calls to blood."

"Maybe. But the king has no magic. Then again, I don't think anybody could compel her – with or without magic. If she comes, she'll come of her own choice, and judging from my past experience, anything is possible. But she is not the sort that likes to be summoned, even if it's only an attempt…"

"I'm a healer, Taingern. It's a chance I'm willing to take. It's the *only* chance we have."

The Durlin ran a hand through his hair. "There's a flaw in your plan though, as well you know."

"Yes, I know. The king is of her blood. But Aranloth is not of hers. She may not be able to recall his spirit as she did long ago for her servant. Yet Aranloth is not just any lòhren. And the queen, even in death, has power."

Taingern closed his eyes. What he was remembering, and he obviously *was* remembering something, etched an expression of awe over all his features.

"Yes, she has power. Even in death, she has power. But she's not like Gilhain. They share the same blood, but she is … she is the *Witch Queen*."

13. The Ancient Past

Gilhain did not expect a let up in the battle. Nor was there one. The horde came again, hurling itself against the Cardurleth, spending its life at the command of the enemy leadership.

And the enemy leadership spent life cheaply. But the horde seemed near endless; no matter how many died, more were sent against the wall. Yet for this much Gilhain could be grateful: there had not as yet been any further sorcerous attacks. Elùgroths had died when their summoning had been destroyed.

He looked down over the battlement. The serpent was still there, twitching now and then in its long death. The enemy must clamber over it when they came to attack, and the reminder of the failure of one of their great hopes would sap their morale. Yet in time the stench of it as it decayed would rise up to the defending soldiers, and it would add yet one more thing to the many that they must endure.

Yet they *would* endure. Pride swelled his heart and tears glistened unexpectedly in his eyes. Everything had been thrown at the defenders, steel and sorcery both, and they still defied the enemy. Live or die, save Cardoroth or fall with it into oblivion, they had earned a place in the history of Alithoras. Their story would be told as long as free people remained in the land.

During lulls the stonemasons worked on the battlement. There were many of them, and soldiers helped also. Bit by bit the Cardurleth took shape again. The merlons were necessary: they offered protection to the archers and soldiers both. Men had died because of their lack, but what the serpent had broken men now repaired. And a will seemed to be growing among them, a spirit that he had never seen before. Nor would he have, for Cardoroth had never been pressed this hard in his lifetime, or for many long generations before.

He saw on the faces of the men a certainty of future death, but he also saw a look of determination. Death would not claim them one week, one day, one hour, nor even one moment sooner than it must. They would fight without stint and bring as many of the enemy with them into oblivion as they could.

Gilhain contemplated the opposing host. The sorcerers who led it must be tired. But so too were the lòhrens. And Aranloth was gone. It was only now that the old man could no longer be seen, leaning on his staff and calmly watching the enemy, that Gilhain realized how much he had leaned on him. He was the king's staff, the crutch for the whole city. And Gilhain missed him.

He felt the small soft hand of his wife slip into his own. She always knew what he was thinking.

They did not speak, but stood watching the enemy as the elug war drums slowed to a near stop, and then began a different beat.

Aurellin tilted her head. "What does *that* mean?"

"I don't know," Gilhain said. "Aranloth would. And I miss him."

"We all miss him. But if he's not here to tell us, then we'll discover it in due course ourselves."

They did not have to wait too long. Within a few moments Aurellin coolly drew the short sword that she had taken to wearing at her side.

"They'll now use what they always hold back – the lethrin."

Gilhain saw straightaway that she was right. The lethrin began to march to the fore of the host. They strode in unison; their towering seven-foot frames dwarfed the elugs. The iron maces they carried were held over their right shoulder, and the precious stones on their black uniforms glinted.

In silence the lethrin strode, singing no marching song nor chanting any war cry, but the stomp of their boots rose up toward the defenders, and it seemed that the ground reverberated with their menacing approach. Fear came before them in a wave, for these were the troops that had taken cities in the past; these were the creatures whose hide-like skin defied edged weapons; these were the shadow-spawned soldiers who slew in silence and made no cry even in death.

They came before the Cardurleth. A hail of arrow shafts greeted them. They bore no shields and wore only silvered mail vests, for they needed little defense. Instead, they now held their maces before them and flicked arrows away with deft movements; too deft for their size, but in these creatures great strength and athletic grace were combined: Gilhain knew that and feared it.

Yet he knew also their weaknesses. Legend spoke of them. Aranloth had discussed it with him. Fire and axes could bring them down.

He gave a signal. Men brought forth vats of oil, stored at the back of the battlement. These they got ready to pour over the wall, and archers prepared special arrows that would be tied with oil-soaked cloth and set afire.

The lethrin ceased their march. They stood ready beneath the wall, but they held no ladders. These were being brought up swiftly behind them now by elugs, and with these ladder-carriers came other elugs. They held wide shields constructed of some sort of metal, though they were thin and easily borne.

This was something new, and Gilhain's mind raced. Swiftly he considered these new things, double the width of a normal shield, and discovered their purpose. They were not foolproof, but they would offer a greater chance to the lethrin climbing the wall. That was where they had often been defeated in the past, for their numbers were never great and by killing them by fire as they climbed the axemen waiting for them would not be overwhelmed. But now this would not work, for the shields would deflect the oil. And it would take many axemen to kill each lethrin.

"We're at risk of being overrun," Gilhain said.

"What's to be done?" Aurellin asked.

"I'm working on it."

At that moment the lethrin did what they had never done before. They raised their heads and in seemingly one voice yelled a single word: *Kardoch!*

Gilhain did not know what it meant. But it filled him with a growing worry. It set the lethrin loose like an arrow sped from a bow and they commenced to run toward the wall. And he still had no plan.

The lethrin were silent once more. Their great strides took them to the base of the Cardurleth, and there, elugs scampering about them, they commenced to climb the ladders brought by their comrades. Up each ladder first went an elug, and each of these lifted one of the strange shields above them. They climbed swiftly for all that they were encumbered, and Gilhain knew they had special straps to help hold the shields to one arm and that also they had spent much time training the maneuver. That could be a good thing, for if they were repelled their morale would sink low. The serpent was destroyed, and if their special surprise method to take the city failed, they would be disheartened.

But Gilhain must first make that happen. And at last he knew what he was going to do. If the oil was of no use thrown over the battlement, he must use it at the top of the Cardurleth itself.

He quickly gave orders and they were carried out all down the defenses to each side.

The lethrin climbed. Up the ladders they came, their long arms hauling them with speed. Their black tunics, trimmed with precious stones, gleamed and sparkled. Their silvered chain mail vests, which left their arms free, glinted. In their mighty hands, though they climbed, they still held their enormous maces.

The defenders were not idle while the lethrin climbed. Some shot arrows or dropped rocks, but these had little effect. Most were repelled by the lead elug on each ladder that held the strange shields. Anything that slipped past them was shrugged aside by the lethrin like an ox merely flicking its ears in annoyance at a fly. But other men carried out a task of greater importance. They ran oil in a line along the entire length of the Cardurleth assailed by the enemy. When they were done, they stepped back.

Gilhain waited. To fire it too soon was to allow the lethrin a warning. To fire it too late was to risk them passing over the lip of the battlement and beyond before the flames took hold.

He gave a signal. A lone horn blew, and men with torches ran forward and dropped them by the score in the oil. Everyone leapt back.

"Now, have hope!" Gilhain said to Aurellin.

The lethrin neared. The shield-bearing elugs came first. Over the rampart they came, and fear came with them for they knew their job was done and that they would die. Yet they were surprised that the defenders had backed away.

Momentarily, hope showed on their faces. Then grim fear again as the flames took to the oil. But the elugs had nowhere to go. The lethrin surged up behind them, forcing them to leap forward like sparkling wine from an uncorked bottle.

The elugs spilled out on the battlement. Flame took them. They screamed. Some tried to jump back over the battlement to end the pain, but the lethrin still drove them forward. There was no retreat that way.

Yet the lethrin paused themselves. They saw the flame, and they feared it. While they paused, men shot at them from only a few feet away with their longbows. Neither their toughened hide nor their chainmail vests were entirely proof against attack at such close range. Some died, but those still coming up from behind pushed them ahead even as these had pushed the elugs.

They jumped through the flames. Their black tunics caught alight. But their great maces rose in their hands and they charged at the defenders.

Gilhain assessed his men. They remained resolute, and pride surged in him. The enemy had thrown everything at them, yet still they held firm. And they held again against the rush of lethrin that now threatened to swamp them.

The lethrin crashed into them, maces swinging, using their size and weight to try to smash all opposition away. But the men fought doggedly, ducking, weaving, avoiding blows and distracting the enemy as best they could while axemen worked their trade.

The axes did little damage, but here and there a lethrin fell. When that happened, they were not allowed up again. It was a grim business.

The battle hung in the balance. The lethrin fought silently. The men fought determinedly. There was no give in either, and yet the fire had not been without effect. It played a small part in the initial rush, but oil splashed up from boots onto skin and clothes. It caught and burned, and it did not go out.

The lethrin began to waver, yet they had driven the men back and soon the enemy would order another charge. If a new wave of attackers reached the wall, the fight would be lost.

Gilhain gave the signal that he had waited for patiently. It was now or never, and it would raise morale and speed the fight, or they were all doomed. He turned to the man behind him, his horn-bearer, who held one of the great carnyx horns. He would lead all the horn-blowers, and all down the line they would blow, perhaps a hundred of them.

The first low note sounded, and the others came to life with it. It was a sound out of the deep reaches of the past, out of the age of heroes. The horns were man high, tall as the tall men who bore them, but they held them up until the brass mouths voiced their unearthly moan twelve feet in the air.

And so unearthly was the slow growing din that thrummed and boomed and bellowed like a wild beast that goosebumps stood out on Gilhain's skin. Here was the same sound that rang in the ears of his ancestors as they fought to survive and eventually found realms. Here was the sound that laid their kings to rest since before Cardoroth was even built, back in the dim days when the Camar dwelled nigh to the lands of the Halathrin, back into even dimmer days before that when they lived on the green plains and in the dark forests west of Halathar.

And the defenders stirred to it. It roiled through their blood. It gave strength to their arms and courage to their hearts. Their axes bit harder. Their eyes burned with the spirit inside them. They fell, but they got up again. They were wounded, but they fought heedless of their injuries. They saw death press at them, but they stared it down.

And the lethrin faltered. This was courage that they had seldom met, and the fire still burned wherever the oil touched them. Their attack wavered, and then for the first time in the history of Alithoras they turned and fled. And the jeers of the defenders went after them.

The enemy horde moaned. Their drums ceased to beat and Gilhain yelled in a high, clear voice. *Cardoroth*!

14. A High Price

For Brand the days passed in a strange blend of ease and tension.

He enjoyed riding with Kareste, but he did not appreciate the feeling of pursuit. Without doubt, the witch was around. If she was as old as she claimed, she would have learned patience if nothing else. He often felt that pinprick tightening of skin on his back that crawled to the top of his scalp – that uneasy sensation of being watched. She was around, and she was waiting, and she would bide her time.

He was confident however that she would not try anything for a while. She did not disturb them, and she made no overt threat. But her presence was a palpable, if remote thing, and he did not like it. It took away from the sense of comradeship that he had with Kareste: that it was just the two of them alone in the wild and beautiful lands of Alithoras.

It was still a peaceful time though, all the more so for the fact that trouble lay ahead. He wanted it to last, to continue and to allow his bond with her to grow, but it would *not* last. Durletha would make another attempt on the staff. Khamdar was likely enough still alive. And ahead of them lay a trial to try to free the Halathrin warriors transformed into fell beasts by dark sorcery.

Each of these things was a challenge on its own that might test them to their limits and defeat them. Together, just surviving seemed an unreachable goal. And behind them all lay Cardoroth and Brand's quest to save it. It felt as though the sky had filled with an ocean of dark water that was about to inundate him forever and draw him into its blackness.

Brand shrugged to himself as he rode. His mistake was to think of these things all together, but in truth they must be broken down and faced one step at a time. Even the greatest challenges could be tackled that way. And right now the only step he needed to concern himself with was finding the Great North Road and the ford that led across the Carist Nien and back into the north of Alithoras.

The river was close by on the right. The long green grass nearby bent low at the touch of a warm wind, and perspiration beaded his face. The river, beyond the band of trees that lined its bank, was a silver ribbon. Long they had followed it, yet they had seen neither its source nor its end. Alithoras was vast, and even Brand, who had seen more than most, realized that what he had seen so far was like a single sand grain on the shores of Lake Alithorin.

"We're getting close," Kareste said.

"How far do you think the witch will follow us?"

Kareste flicked the end of her reins at a fly that kept trying to land on her hand.

"What do *you* think?"

"Well, I guess I know the answer. But I was hoping you'd prove me wrong."

She grinned at him, catching his little barb. "I can be a bit like that."

In truth, he had no hope at all that Durletha would ever give up, but he knew so little about her.

"Is she really as old as she claimed?"

Kareste frowned. "I'm not sure. I don't really know much about her, but there's mention of her in the lore of the lòhrens."

She seemed to consider this as she rode, reaching back in thought or memory to something learned long ago.

"She probably told the truth about her age, but there are others beside her. She's not the only creature of magic that wanders Alithoras, or abides in remote and secret places. There are many powers besides lòhrens and elùgroths, some older and some younger. Some are aligned to the Light, and some to the Shadow, but most stay hidden and pursue their own goals. Some are quite strange, but they do us no harm."

"The world is a strange place," he said.

"Truly," she agreed. She became thoughtful then, and after a few moments chanted softly:

Many things lie
Beneath the sky
Beyond the ken
Of mortal men.

Brand looked at her quizzically.

"It's an old rhyme of lòhren lore," she explained. "There are many such snatches of verse, and there's truth embedded in them."

Not long after they came to the Great North Road. Brand still thought about what she had said of the other powers in Alithoras, and he wondered yet again what her final allegiance would be, to the Light or to the Shadow. He did not really believe in anything in between. And then he began to question himself as he had done ever since they escaped the tombs of the Letharn: was he right not to try to talk to her and influence her decision?

As always, he came to the same conclusion – it was better not to. His best option was to lead by example, if he could. Actions spoke louder than words, and people had a habit of doing the opposite of whatever someone tried to talk them into.

They neared the ford where the road crossed the river. The sun-bleached sky was pale, yet he saw a speck wheeling far away and high up. He had the feeling it was a hawk, that it was Durletha, though of that he could not be sure. It was nothing more than intuition. But Kareste had become subdued, and he guessed that she sensed the same thing that he did.

The rush and gurgle of the ford was loud.

"I'm not sure that I want to cross here," he said.

"Nor I. Yet there's nowhere else."

That was true, but it did not mean that he had to like it.

They moved ahead warily. Here, the trees that usually banded the river gave way to deep drifts of sand and to coarse gravel. And there were boulders and hollowed out pits where rushing water had gouged the ground. It was all in the open, and yet there were many places that people could hide.

The mighty river was wide here, so wide that the far bank seemed a long way away, and yet the frothy water flowed and bubbled as though the riverbed were only a foot or so below its sun-glinting surface. But closer than the far bank, perhaps half way across, was a little island of sand and driftwood. The Great North Road ran straight and true, and there were signs of it even on the island.

Brand was in no hurry. He waited and watched, and Kareste did the same beside him. His feeling of unease grew, though he saw no sign of anything disturbing.

The silence built. The only sound was that of the river, and far away the high-pitched call of the wheeling hawk. Insects flickered through the humid air, drawn to the water, and a fish leaped high and quick in search of a meal, and then dropped back with a splash into the river.

Eventually, there was movement. A man emerged from behind one of the boulders halfway down the slope to the river's edge.

The man was scar-faced and grim. He was tall, his black hair long and lank. His clothes seemed strange, a patchwork of items gathered here and there, none of them clean. A sword was belted at his side, and there was a lump here and there in his clothing where other weapons were likely hidden. Beneath thick brows his eyes were narrow and dark. Brand read meanness there, or worse, but the man tried to mask his natural features with a pretense of friendliness.

"Well met, fellow travelers."

Brand inclined his head slightly, but he did not take his eyes off the man.

"Hello," he said in a voice that was friendly but not especially encouraging of further conversation.

"Where are you going?"

"Just passing through," Brand answered. He was attempting to be as short as he possibly could without being rude. He did not wish to start anything here, but he knew that the choice of that was not likely going to be his.

The man showed a flicker of irritation, but he soon covered it. His strategy, and Brand *knew* it was a strategy, was to lull suspicion by friendly talk. He was not alone. Others remained hidden, and there was going to be trouble.

"Perhaps you have some food to share with someone who hasn't eaten in days?" The man said awkwardly. He had been forced to come to the point more quickly than he wished.

Brand had seen the starved and the hungry before. Faces came to him out of the past, before he had come to Cardoroth. This man was neither of those things. Still, generosity was never a bad thing, and he would do whatever could be done to avoid a fight.

"A little," he answered, with a quick warning look to Kareste. "We're willing to share what we have."

"Then come down by the river," Scarface said. "It's cool near the water."

There was a pause, and Brand made no move. "Come up and join us."

Scarface did not answer. There was a longer pause this time, and his expression slowly changed. The pretense of friendliness dropped away as he realized that he had not fooled the two travelers.

"Come out, boys," he said over his shoulder. "They're on to us. Not that it'll help them."

Men came out of their hiding spots. Some were concealed in the declivities; some behind boulders. Several even emerged from the water. They would have been set there as a last resort in case the riders sped through before any trap could be properly sprung.

Brand noted that some of the men *did* indeed look hungry. But not Scarface, nor those who came to stand closest to him. Some were well armed and dressed, but he was pleased that none carried bows.

Scarface spoke when his men had gathered around him.

"It's food we want, but we'll take everything else as well." His grin turned to a leer when he looked at Kareste.

Brand wondered what the man would think if he knew of the massive diamond that was stashed away in one of his saddlebags. It was a kingly gift from Gilhain; and a gift that Brand had no intention of losing to the likes of Scarface and his men. Yet he and Kareste must cross the ford.

In the silence that ensued, Scarface spoke again. "Most especially, I like your helm and sword."

Brand looked at him coolly. When he answered, his voice was neutral. He did not wish to provoke anything here if it could be avoided.

"Both those items come at a high price."

Scarface laughed. "I have men enough to help me pay. More than enough."

Brand studied them with a casual glance. "No, you don't."

15. It will be a Long Night

The carnyx horns sang their unearthly song. It ran through Gilhain's blood and made him feel young again. The retreat of the enemy buoyed him, and he held Aurellin's hand. It was good to be alive, and though there could be no such thing as winning the war against an enemy that overpowered them, no one and nobody could take away this victory, no matter that it would be short lived.

He felt a sense of overwhelming love. Aurellin's hand in his felt warm and soft, and it was a bridge for the love that existed between them. They needed no words, no glance, and in truth did not even need to hold hands to express their feeling for each other. Gilhain felt it in the very air around him just by her presence, and he knew that she felt the same. But it was still nice to hold hands.

"They'll come again. And soon," she said softly.

"I know," he answered. "I would do the same in their position. They cannot let their troops ponder the defeat of the lethrin for long – that would sap morale. They must now throw everything they can against us to distract their own from defeat, and to show us that no matter how many times we throw them back, they'll come again. By doing that they'll sap our own morale."

Aurellin nodded. "But is it possible to undermine the morale of an army that already acknowledges its ultimate defeat, and fights anyway?"

Gilhain considered that. It was a good question. While he thought, he saw the first movements of the enemy.

"That, we shall soon see," he replied.

Aurellin did not answer. She watched as did he, as did all the defenders, while a great wave of elugs came from the horde and surged toward the wall. Fear came before them, and among them were some of the lethrin who still lived, shamed by their earlier retreat and eager to regain their prestige as invincible warriors. But the defenders now knew that they were not, and fighting was always played out in the mind before ever a blow landed.

The enemy crashed against the wall. The war drums thrashed. Up the elugs climbed; down were cast rocks and spears, and swift were the hissing arrows of the archers dispensed.

On came the enemy. Ladders were toppled. Climbing ropes were severed. But still they came in a seething mass, intent on reaching the top and destroying all that Gilhain loved.

The enemy crested the Cardurleth like a flood. Driven by sorcery or fear, compelled by their masters, they would not retreat this time. Either they were killed, or all would fall beneath their onslaught.

The men met them. Sword crashed against sword. Cries filled the air. Red blood flowed, and the glint of weapons flashed like a thousand wicked suns.

The great maces of the lethrin smashed all before them, but they were few and the elugs many. Yet the many filled the gaps the few provided, and together they pushed back the defenders, inch by inch.

There was no respite. There was no mercy. Even in the long course of the siege there had never been a fight as this: desperate beyond desperation, filled with a vicious kill or be killed attitude that made all else that had gone before it seem as a game.

The enemy seemed possessed, and well they might be. Gilhain wished that Aranloth were here, but he was not. A quick glance along the Cardurleth showed that the lòhrens held back. If this fight was going to be won by the defenders, force of arms and courage of heart alone would achieve it.

The noise was deafening. Cries of fear and pain melded with the clash of blades and the tramp of boots. Over and above that the elug war drums vied with the carnyx horns. The din of it all together was hideous.

But the horror before Gilhain's eyes was worse. The stone was thick with gore. There seemed to be so much that it looked like the heavens had opened and rained blood. And through it were severed limbs and dead bodies and the innards of men and elugs spilled into the bright sunlight. The slaughterhouse of the Cardurleth was grotesque.

But the smell that assaulted his nose was perhaps even worse. He retched. The stench was near overpowering, and battle-hardened though he was, he had not experienced its like before.

Yet beside him Aurellin looked on, her face a mask that hid her feelings. He *knew* she felt as he did, but there was steel in her. And whatever she felt she kept it in one part of her mind and allowed another to assess the battle dispassionately. And so must he.

Things hung in the balance. No battle could long continue at this ferocity. One side must soon gain the advantage. And the defenders were being pushed back. More and more elugs came to the wall, and when one fell, two took its place. Yet the lethrin, now few in number, were not immune to death. They fell and died, though it took many men to bring them down. While the men did this, the elugs gathered about them in their turn and killed them.

Gilhain wondered what he could do next. Had the time come to wield his own blade? Could he rally the defenders by joining the fray? Yet there was risk in that, for the enemy would be drawn to him like moths to a flame: if they killed him the heart would go out of the defense.

He fingered the hilt of his sword. Then Aurellin put a hand on his shoulder.

"Wait," she mouthed, for her voice would not carry above the screaming mayhem of battle.

He followed her gaze, for though her hand was on his shoulder she did not look at him.

A large man caught his eye. He was part of a group that surged forward against the enemy. But the group was soon hammered down by the broad sweeps of a lethrin mace and the quick stabs of elugs that darted in and out, swords flashing, in their massive companion's wake.

But the man had not fallen. Alone now, and nearly as massive as the lethrin, he strode forward, his eyes bent on his great adversary with grim determination.

Gilhain did not know who the man was. He was just an ordinary soldier. But there was an air to his movements, in the intent look on his face, that signaled that something extraordinary was about to happen, and the hair prickled all the way up the back of the king's neck.

The man threw down his blade. It rang against the stones and shattered. Hundreds of eyes turned to him, and hundreds more when his mighty voice boomed out.

"Fight me!" the big man called, and his challenge rose above the mad din of the battle.

The elugs darted in to kill him, but he shrugged them aside, his mail protecting him from the worst of their blows.

He went straight for the lethrin. The lethrin raised high his mace. As a thunderbolt it fell, hurtling through the air, but the big man was quicker than he looked. With a slight move, only just enough, he stepped to the side. The mace smashed into the stone and sent chips flying, but the big man was moving again.

Incredibly, the lone soldier reached out with his meaty hands and grappled with the lethrin. One hand pinned the arm that held the mace, the other gripped the creature's throat like a vice.

There the two of them stood and strained against each other. The elugs began to land blows against the man, but he ignored them. And then an archer let fly arrows that sang through the air and stuck in several elug throats in the space of two heartbeats.

The elugs hunkered down. The man and the lethrin continued their struggle alone. The great creature tried to raise his mace, but the man held his arm pinned with a strength that Gilhain did not think a man could possess. All the while the breathing of the creature grew labored, and what air it could get whistled in loud rasping gulps down its throat.

The lethrin hammered his other arm against the man, smashing his fist into head and body, but the helmet and mail offered some protection, and grimly the man endured the blows. Soon the lethrin turned instead to trying to prize away the death grip from his throat, but nothing loosed it.

Eventually, the lethrin dropped the mace. He could not bring it to bear, but by letting go of its great weight he now had a better chance to lift up his pinned arm. This he did, slowly but surely, reaching up to try to break the grip that suffocated him.

But the man, not quite able to match strength for strength, was not done yet. He swiftly changed his grip, letting go of both throat and arm, and then in one swift motion he shuffled closer and took the lethrin in a bear hug.

There the two combatants stood. The man tightened his grip. The lethrin rained mighty blows upon him with both fists. Bright blood ran from beneath the soldier's helmet, and then the helm flew loose from his head revealing a shock of red hair and a battered face, swollen and cut.

The two of them staggered back and forth beneath the strain of the forces they brought to bear.

"Watch!" hissed Aurellin.

Gilhain could not have taken his eyes off the scene even if he had wanted to, but he felt the first inkling of an idea of what would happen next, just as had she, and time seemed to slow.

The lethrin drove the man back a step, but the man was not beaten. As he retreated he sunk his weight lower, and then, incredibly, beyond the anticipation of all but a few, he heaved the lethrin off the ground.

There he stood a moment, his legs near buckling under enormous strain. The battle all around had ceased and it seemed as though the struggle between the opposing masses was now centered on the two combatants alone.

And then the man staggered forward, still holding the lethrin above the ground, ignoring the blows landed upon him by the desperate creature.

He tottered forward, his grip unbreakable, and drove the lethrin into a section of the battlement wall that was not yet repaired.

The lethrin ceased his useless striking and took the man in a headlock. For just a moment, as the creature's arms moved, Gilhain glimpsed the beaten face of the soldier. It was a bloody mess, and the flesh around the eyes had swollen so much that Gilhain doubted the man could even see any more.

There the soldier stood for several long moments. The stonework crumbled. A crack ran through it, and all the while the man not only held the lethrin up, but also continued to drive forward with his failing strength.

With a final heave the man pushed the lethrin through the crumbling wall. He knew what would happen. He knew, and the lethrin soon realized it. The massive creature screamed, perhaps the first of his normally silent kind to voice terror atop the walls of a besieged city.

Slowly, surely, inexorably they tumbled over together, locked in their embrace. The man was silent. The fear-filled bellow of the lethrin invoked a sense of sympathy – even among the defenders. But Gilhain's thoughts were mostly of the brave soldier, now slipped from sight. Who was he? Was he married? Where had such courage come from?

But Gilhain knew the battle hung in the balance, and he had no time for sentimentality. The soldier had chosen his own time to die, now Gilhain must use that sacrifice to save his people a little longer, for he saw now how it could be done.

The battle had come to a standstill. Men, elugs and lethrin stood in shock. Gilhain was the first to act. He signaled quickly for the carnyx horns to start again – they had fallen silent. But without waiting he leaped toward the enemy taking all by surprise, even the Durlin who stood near.

His great sword swung. Blood flowed. Elugs died, and he cried *Cardoroth!* at every stroke of his blade. The defenders saw their king smite the enemy, and they followed suit. Courage swelled their hearts, and dismay fell upon their opponents. They could not believe what they had just witnessed, and they could not rally.

The defenders drove into them. They pushed them back. The windrows of dead and dying lay thick on the battlement; the living were caught between a plunging death behind them and a storm of flashing blades ahead of them.

The king was not alone. Aurellin was with him, her own short sword slicing and stabbing, and around them, trying their best to protect them, were the Durlin.

The white surcoats of the Durlin were stained with blood. But none of it was theirs. They slew with skill and speed that astonished even Gilhain, and the enemy fled before them, fighting among themselves to find the ropes and climb down the battlement to safety.

But the ropes were few, and elugs were climbing up them from below. None escaped that way. The swords of the defenders cut them down until none were left save those starting to climb, and these began to turn and flee.

Gilhain looked along the Cardurleth. It was the same elsewhere. The enemy had been routed once more, and yet it had come at a price.

Men hurled the dead bodies of the elugs over the wall. They piled down below, burying the serpent. Gilhain wondered if the enemy intended to build a ramp of their own dead in order to reach the top of the wall. They had the numbers to do it. But in any civilized war, if there was such a thing, the besieging army would take away their dead at prearranged times without fear of being shot by arrows. But the enemy had made no such request of Gilhain. Rather, their leadership preferred to use the stench as a weapon, hoping to make the defenders uncomfortable, no matter that it did the same to their own soldiers and provided a breeding ground for disease.

But the enemy dead were not the only ones. Brave soldiers of Cardoroth had died also – by the hundreds. There were too many to be taken away all at once, and the dead lay there, their eyes vacant, and in their exhaustion the defenders who yet lived sat down beside them. At times it was hard to tell who was alive and who was dead. And though they had just now won a great victory, it could not go on like this indefinitely. Cardoroth was a big city, but it could not match the enemy soldier for soldier. They must not take so many losses in the future.

All the while the wild carnyx horns had been blowing. If they were eerie before, they were more so now in the sudden silence after the enemy's retreat. Now, however, the horns took up a new note. It was only a subtle difference, but there was in it a hint of victory. And well the army deserved it; they had fought for it and it was pleasing to see the enemy, a disorganized mass, heads low, officers barking orders, faces sullen and most of all – the hateful elug war drums gone quiet.

The enemy host was at its lowest ebb yet. Had he the numbers, Gilhain would have ordered a sortie, for there was no better time than now to strike.

He sighed. He did not have the numbers. Instead, he must simply watch as the enemy regrouped and then came back at them again. But at least the defenders would have that same time as a respite.

He leaned on his bloody sword, Aurellin standing near. There was still a fierce look on her face, and after all these years she still surprised him. There was steel in her; that he had always known, but it was a thing of the mind and not of the body. At least so he had thought. Yet she had propelled herself into the fray and wielded her blade with ferocity. She had no great skill, yet she had killed, and the sight of her fighting beside their king had lent strength to the defenders.

There was a noise in the silence behind him. Taingern had returned. His face was grim, though whether because of what he saw atop the Cardurleth or for news of Aranloth, Gilhain did not know.

"You look tired," Taingern said.

Gilhain cleaned his sword on a rag. "It's been a long day."

Taingern looked him in the eye. "I'm sorry, my King, but it will be a long night also."

Gilhain sheathed the blade. "How so?"

"Arell has discovered a way to attempt a healing of Aranloth."

"What way is that?"

Taingern's gaze did not falter. "You won't like it."

16. The Forgotten Queen

They were atop the tower, the Tower of Halathgar, the Witch Queen's tower, and Gilhain felt uneasy.

The attacking horde had withdrawn to lick its wounds when dusk fell. Their campfires sprang to light, the vast host gathering in and enveloping itself in its pain.

They were unnaturally quiet, for their great attack of sorcery had been foiled – the serpent lay dead, or still dying, and the great charge of the lethrin had been repulsed. Yet the leadership, both sorcerers and shazrahads, those strange men from the south, would work through the night. Tomorrow, the host would attack again. And if their confidence had diminished, it would grow again over time. In a day, or a week, the enemy would be ravening for blood once more.

But for a time, Gilhain could put that concern aside. For a few brief hours something else would hold his attention. And though there were no armies up here at the summit of the tower, though there would be no fighting, what was about to happen was just as important as any battle played out on the Cardurleth. Possibly more so.

It was dark. Yet the crows in the trees croaked and flapped their wings. Perhaps the men holding flaming torches disturbed them. Perhaps it was something else.

Gilhain looked out over the parapet. He could see little of the park where the trees grew; shadows lay thick over it like drifts of black fog. Like fog, the shadows moved too. Or something within them did, but it was too far away and too dark to see.

Further away he saw the torch-lit city, for here at the top of this tower he was high, high enough to feel a cool breeze blowing against the cold sweat that slicked the skin of his face. There was no breeze down below.

He heard a muffled curse. "Careful," Arell said to the Durlin who carried Aranloth's stretcher.

It had been hard work to get the stretcher all the way up the stairs, for there were few people here. Gilhain wanted it that way, and all that he allowed were the Durlin, himself, Aurellin and of course Arell. They all spoke in hushed tones. Some knew what was to be attempted up here, but even those who did not sensed that something strange and unusual was in the air.

Gilhain smiled to himself. Strange and unusual did not even begin to cover it. Carnhaina, better known as the Witch Queen, sometimes called the Forgotten Queen, was his foremother. Near on a thousand years had passed since her rule of Cardoroth, and though the general population had forgotten her except for a few strange stories and ballads that were told late at night in inns, his family had not. She was venerated by all of his line, and every subsequent king or queen of Cardoroth had lived in her shadow, for she had achieved great things. And now, more than ever, he felt unworthy of his heritage, for it seemed likely enough that the city would fall despite his best efforts. And it was not remembered that Carnhaina was forgiving.

Gilhain glanced over at the sarcophagus that held her remains. Few knew that this was her resting place, here in her tower atop its parapet, beneath the light of the constellation of bright Halathgar. He fingered the hilt of the knife he carried, the same one that he had given to Brand, the same one that the elùgroth had hurled at him. It was marked with the constellation, marked with the queen's sign.

112

He looked at Aranloth on the stretcher. His face was gray, and he was near death. The crows flapped raucously in the trees. Taingern was somber and distant.

Taingern. He was a man who had been here before, and he had an idea of what to expect, assuming that anything at all would happen. Gilhain had been here himself; there were certain rituals involved in the coronation of a king, and though that was long ago he remembered it well. Yet the queen had never appeared to him. But she *had* appeared to Brand and Taingern, had summoned their help to thwart a sorcerer who would rob her tomb. Would she appear now? Was there merit to Arell's wild scheme? Was there truth in the dim legend that had come down from his forefathers that Carnhaina, even in death, guarded the city and that she would return in its darkest hour? He would soon find out, but what he knew of her, what he had learned from Brand, made him wonder if he wanted her to appear at all.

He steeled himself. He must do this for Aranloth's sake. And for Cardoroth as well, whatever his personal fears.

"It's time," Aurellin whispered in his ear.

Gilhain stirred. He saw that Arell was looking at him. The stretcher was laid out next to the sarcophagus. The Durlin had stepped away.

Gilhain walked forward. He gave a sign and Taingern used a metal bar to lever, ever so carefully, the stone lid off the casket.

Stone grinded on stone. The crows flapped and cawed, some taking clumsily to the air to circle the tower.

It seemed to take forever, but eventually Taingern was done and the lid was moved half off. There he stopped, and the king noted that the Durlin did not look inside.

Gilhain hesitated, and Arell came to his side. She must have sensed what he would keep hidden. "There's no other way," she said.

He nodded and suppressed his fear. *That* he could overcome, but the thought that Carnhaina may hold him responsible for the looming fall of her city was something that he could not suppress. And well she might hold him so, and such a rebuke might break him.

He drew the knife. Her knife. The blade that had come down through long generations to him.

He stepped closer to the sarcophagus. The breeze died, and the crows grew still. Stars glittered overhead with a cold light. He looked over the stone edge and gazed within.

He saw bones; pale in the starlight, broken and fragmented. The flesh of the queen's body, laid to rest in antiquity, had decayed to dust. The skull, white and stark, glared back at him; under its dislodged jaw rested a torc, its twisted gold gleaming bright. Jewels and coins and rings and treasures of a lost age winked at him, colder than the stars.

"Hear me," Gilhain said. His voice was a croak, and the words seemed empty high up at the top of the tower, almost as though the dark night all around swallowed them.

"Hear me!" he said, suddenly loud. "I, Gilhain, King of Cardoroth, have come. I, who am descended from thy line, seek audience. I, Gilhain, summon thee!"

With a deft move he held up the palm of his left hand and sliced with the blade in his right. He did it quickly, else he knew he would have trouble to do it at all.

He felt nothing, but the blade was sharp and in a moment his bright blood flew. It spattered over the bones and the skull. Then the pain began. It stung, and then it ached, and then it sent a stabbing pain through him. He ignored it.

"Hear me, Carnhaina! Hear me, my Queen! I summon thee. Blood calls to blood. Come, for Cardoroth needs you. Hear me, and come!"

He ceased speaking. It was deathly quiet. Nothing happened. The pain in his palm grew. It throbbed. He felt it like a creeping thing that gripped his hand and squeezed, and then it moved up his arm and to his whole body until he trembled in agony.

The crows in the park now clamored madly, and the cold breeze fluttered to life once more. The dust at the bottom of the sarcophagus, that once had been living flesh, seethed. An ethereal shape formed and rose in a swirl of color and Gilhain and Arell stumbled back.

The vision of a woman stood tall and stately before them. She gazed at those atop the tower, her eyes terrible and stern. They were blue, a deep and cold shade that Gilhain had never seen before, but her skin was pale and freckled, and her unbound hair shone like spilled blood. Wild curls, thick and lustrous, ran down the length of her back and shimmered at the touch of the night-dark air.

She was a massive figure, heavy-boned, thick-limbed and large-jawed. The gold torc he had seen in the sarcophagus gleamed brilliantly about her neck, and about her body was cast a cloak of many colors. In her right hand she grasped an iron-headed spear as though ready to strike.

Her cold stare bored into Gilhain. "Who dares wake me?"

Gilhain bowed. As king, he bowed to none, but he could not help himself, such was the awe that mantled her.

"I, Gilhain, King of Cardoroth, Lord of the Camar, Ruler of the North—"

"Halt!" the queen commanded. "I know you and have heard those titles before. Once I bore them, and others beside. But when you are dust you will learn how empty they are. Speak! Why have you dared to disturb me?"

Gilhain grew in confidence. He had not summoned her, he had not the power. But she had come anyway, and she sought to hide the fact that it had been willingly. Thus he believed that it was possible that she might help.

"Cardoroth is in great need. A host besieges us—"

"This I know. I am dead, but I am not stupid."

Gilhain was unprepared for this. That Carnhaina had been a difficult woman in life, he knew. But how to deal with her, how to deal with a long-dead spirit and try to negotiate her help, was beyond even his wide experience. Still, he straightened and spoke with directness.

"The city will fall. Elugs we can, perhaps, withstand. But not sorcerers. Lòhrens we have on the walls, but the greatest of them lies dying beside you. His spirit is sped from his body, and I would have you call him back. Without his aid, Cardoroth is lost."

Carnhaina did not look at Aranloth. She knew he was there. She knew why they had come. She knew each of them atop the tower and read their innermost hearts. She exchanged a brief look with Taingern, and a smile flashed from her eyes, and then in an instant she was stern again.

Her glance fell on Gilhain once more and he shivered.

"Plans rarely run true," she said. "You see the death of Aranloth as your greatest problem, but what if I told you that Brand has obtained the second half of Shurilgar's staff? What if I told you that he has not destroyed it, and now the Shadow comes for him? All now stands in jeopardy, and even if Aranloth lived he could not help the greater cause."

That hit Gilhain as a blow, but he did not hesitate to answer.

116

"Maybe so, yet still could he help Cardoroth, and I would have it so!"

She raised an eyebrow at him, and he did not think she was dissatisfied with his answer. For the first time she looked at the lòhren, and her face was unreadable.

Surprisingly, it was Arell who spoke. "Why hasn't Brand destroyed the staff? He wouldn't betray us, so there's some reason you haven't said."

The queen's glance fell on the healer, but Arell returned the cool gaze without flinching.

"He seeks now to save a soul. One soul while a city of people is on the brink. Once, I would have called such an act wrong. Now, I do not know. But I will tell you this – he seeks to save the soul of a girl. He travels with her. Does that upset you?"

Arell did not answer, and Carnhaina spoke into the silence.

"Yes it does. You see much, but I see more. You cannot hide your thoughts from me. You would be with him in her stead. And truly, that might be better for Alithoras. But not even the dead see all ends."

Carnhaina dropped her gaze down to the stretcher and looked at Aranloth again. The breeze gusted and flared her hair in a shimmer of red, but the queen gave no sign that she felt it.

"Have you considered," she said, turning back to Gilhain, "that of all who ever lived, Aranloth has most need to die – to leave toil and struggle and sorrow beyond endurance behind? Anyway, it is of no matter. I cannot recall him."

Gilhain was dismayed. It must have showed on his face, for his foremother looked at him and raised an eyebrow.

"This surely you knew? He is too far gone. The blood of kin recalled me, but the lòhren is not related. Blood alone is not enough. It would take more, much more than blood for me to even attempt it."

A cold feeling settled in the pit of Gilhain's stomach. Aurellin tensed beside him.

"What *would* it take?" The words were a dry whisper in his throat.

"When blood does not suffice, a life might avail. But not any life. It must be the sacrifice of a king."

Gilhain did not move. He had known that was coming, as had Aurellin. And both of them knew what his answer would be. She said nothing and did not try to dissuade him. She merely put her hand in his and squeezed. It was such a small movement, but he felt a world of love in the gesture, and it was all he could do to stifle the tears ready to spring to his eyes.

There was utter silence. He gave Aurellin's hand a squeeze of his own, and then reluctantly let go and took a pace forward. He did not speak, but turned around the knife he still held in his hand and offered it to Carnhaina, hilt first.

The queen looked at it curiously. And then she laughed. Gilhain wondered if she was not a little mad. She made no move to take the blade, but suddenly she stood taller and the smile left her face. Terrible and stern she seemed. Her fingers gripped tight the spear shaft that she held in her right hand. She looked up at the sky, and Gilhain knew she was looking at Halathgar, that constellation of two bright points whose semblance she must have seen on the knife. He guessed it was his imagination, but it seemed to him that the light of the real stars glittered in her eyes and sparked off the iron-tipped spear.

A moment she stood like that, and he did not move. The Durlin, however, stepped closer. With a glance at

Taingern he stilled them. His life, for the possibility of Aranloth's, was a good exchange.

A wispy cloud dimmed the starlight, and a shadow passed over the top of the tower. He blinked, and when he looked at Carnhaina again he found that she was gazing at him, and her face was unreadable.

"You are a fit king," she said. "Thus do you pass the test. Put the knife away and watch, for I am Carnhaina, and once the world trembled at my power!"

The queen leaned forward, and she reached through the stone of her sarcophagus as though it were not there. With the tip of the spear she pricked the lòhren's flesh twice. Two bright spots of blood blossomed on his robes near his heart.

The air grew chill. Cold starlight glittered on the blood-wetted spear-point. It gleamed on Carnhaina's torc. Her eyes grew fierce, and her meaty hands wrapped around the ash-wood shaft.

"Aranloth!" called the queen. "Hear me, lòhren. Hear me, priest of the Letharn who are gone. Hear me, prince of the race who are no more. Hear me, and come!"

Thus she stood, spear in hand, and her eyes flashed with power. Yet Aranloth did not move. The blood darkened on his robes, and the queen hissed.

She raised her arms high, and the star-shadow of the spear leapt from the parapet and into the night. "Come!" she commanded, and even Gilhain, who possessed no magic, felt the force of her will. It thrummed through the tower and reached out, out into the night, out over all the land and into an oblivion so vast that he recoiled from the sense of it.

But Carnhaina did not recoil. She was one with it. Her voice filled it, and her mind encompassed it, seeking the spirit of the one she called.

119

Gilhain shook his head. This was more than he expected, perhaps even more than what Carnhaina herself had expected. He had been willing to give his life to recall the lòhren, but now he wondered if any force on earth had that power.

17. The Head of the Snake

Brand did not move. But at a signal from Scarface his men drew their weapons and spread out. The situation was clear: the trap of the bandits had failed, but likewise the two travelers were mounted; they could retreat at any time – unless there was some reason they must cross the ford. And obviously they still intended to, otherwise they would already have turned and galloped away.

Scarface smiled, and Brand felt a sudden wave of intense dislike for the man. Yet he pushed it down. There might still be a chance of getting through this without a fight.

"There are only two of us," Brand said. "But we're mounted. If it comes to a fight, blood will be shed. And some of it will be yours. That is certain. But if it's food you want, we're willing to share what we have. No blood need be spilled. No harm need be done to anyone."

Scarface smirked at him. "The more you talk, the more I know that you need to cross. I don't know why. Perhaps there are other men after you, though I had thought the wild lands south of the river empty of people. But all that really matters is that you want to cross, and you will need to pay to do so."

Brand spoke calmly. "There will be a price paid by you as well. But there—"

"Enough!" Scarface yelled. "Turn and flee. Otherwise, lay down your sword and helm. And leave your horse behind. That way, if you're so concerned about our welfare, you can avoid bloodshed. We promise to let you walk away, free and with your life, but the girl will stay with us."

Brand looked at them all coolly. He knew their type, but there was some darker shadow on them. Something drove them, and his glance flicked to the dot that wheeled in the sky. He understood what was happening, and though these bandits were murderers, he did not doubt that the will of the witch was also on them. There was no way forward without a fight. Men might die, but he must avoid that at all costs. He must show mercy and use his skill only as a last resort. The eyes of all these men were on him, but so too was the silent gaze of Kareste. He must show her that there were better ways than violence, that the darkness in the hearts of men did not always prevail.

He did not speak to Scarface, but to his men. "This is no way to live," he said, "to waylay travelers and accost women. If your leader doesn't see sense, then get yourself a new leader. You can have food for free, but everything else will cost you blood, and some will die. Is it worth it?"

The men did not answer. They looked at him darkly, and once again he felt the will of the witch at work. Without her, without Scarface among them, these men might have seen reason.

"You have your answer," Scarface said.

Brand had tried reason. Now, he would try threat.

"It's not too late to back away. Leave now while you can. I can fight. I can fight well, and I wear armor and wield a sword the likes of which you have never seen."

He drew his blade. The pattern-welded steel shimmered in the bright light, and he heard several gasps. These men would not have seen a Halathrin-forged blade before, but they still recognized it.

"I'm no ordinary warrior. I have skill beyond anything you have encountered. If you come against me I will kill you, each and every one. I do not say this to boast. I say it to save your lives. Stand aside and let us pass, and live another day."

A few of the men wavered, but not enough. Many looked to Scarface, but he stood there, sure of himself, hatred burning in his eyes. The band made no move to part.

Brand dismounted and handed his reins to Kareste. She looked at him strangely, but said nothing.

The Halathrin blade gleamed in his right hand, and he placed Aranloth's staff on the ground with his left.

"Even yet, it's not too late," he said. "I'll fight your leader, one on one, and you'll see that it's better just to let us pass. There need be no more blood shed than that."

Scarface laughed. "The only blood to be shed will be your own."

Brand looked at him coldly. "That's easy to say, surrounded by your men. Step away from them and face me."

Brand was trying his hardest to keep things just between him and Scarface. The leader was the head of the snake, and if he was killed the rest would lose heart. But Scarface knew it too. He spat contemptuously, and with an abrupt gesture signaled his men forward.

Kareste spoke for the first time. "Kill them, Brand. You've tried everything else, now kill them all."

The men paid her no heed, but her words made Brand tremble. They were cold. Colder than he had ever heard her speak before, and he knew that he must still try to avoid bloodshed. He must do something special here, but it would come at great risk.

Brand smiled at the men who stepped slowly toward him. They followed their orders, but they were in no hurry. It gave him time to reach into his saddlebag and pull out the diamond Gilhain had given him. He casually dropped it on the ground at his feet. It shone and sparkled, and the men stood still, their shocked silence absolute.

But Kareste was not so quiet. A gasp escaped her lips, for she had travelled far with him and never knew that he carried such a great treasure.

Now was the moment to act, and Brand timed it to perfection. He waited for the nearest man to blink before he moved. It was the smallest of advantages, so small that an ordinary warrior could not make it work for him. But he was Brand of the Duthenor, and his skill had been honed since childhood and ripened by his service as bodyguard to a much-threatened king.

One moment he stood there, the sword held loosely in his hand, and the next he sprang forward and bridged the gap quicker than the thought or reflex of his opponent. He could have killed him before the man even realized what was happening, but he did not. Instead, he struck with the flat of his blade, cracking it into the other man's hand. Bones broke, and the bandit's rusty sword fell from his shattered hand as he fell backward.

Brand did not hesitate. He wheeled among the outlaws, spinning and leaping. The sword flashed, but it never drew blood. At times he struck with a fist into an opponent's neck, sending them to the ground gasping for air. At other times he kicked, low and swift, striking at groin or knee.

Men fell around him. One toppled and groaned after another kick, and Brand knew that man would never father children. Swords flashed at him, but they only cut the air where he had been. Once, a blade glanced off his helm. There was a ringing noise and a flash of pale light as though sparks flew, but then he felled the man with a blow to his temple from the pommel of his Halathrin sword.

Six men were disabled, felled or falling to the ground before the other six could rally. The initial surprise of

Brand's attack was gone, and now the bandits tried to circle him.

For the first time, steel rang on steel as he parried blows. He slipped among them, swifter than they, but one blade against many. Yet the Halathrin blade was of a quality so far beyond the others that when it struck them, they shattered. Steel shards flew. Daggers were drawn, and they drove through the air, but Brand's mail shirt protected him.

Yet still he began to bleed. Several times he had been cut on wrist and arm. But several more men lay on the ground, knocked out by the pommel of Brand's sword. Momentum was with him, and fear pumped through the remaining bandits who still stood upright. They backed away.

Brand knew he must now make a choice. Scarface, never having joined in the fight, backed away with his men. But if he was left alone, left free to continue as he had started, other travelers, less prepared than Brand had been, would die. Brand did not lower his sword. Should he kill Scarface? If he did, the band would probably fall apart and go their separate ways. But what effect would killing him have on Kareste?

But Scarface was not yet done. He tried surprise as Brand had done. The retreat was only an act, for he drew a dagger and flung it with all his might. It spun through the air, wheeling and glinting, but it did not strike its target.

Brand was already moving. The knife whooshed through the air, but he was a little to its side and moving forward. Before Scarface could react the Halathrin blade slid into him, drove deep, and then came out the man's back.

Scarface tensed. Blood gushed from his mouth and then he collapsed. Quickly, Brand tried to withdraw his sword, but it did not come out as easily as it had gone in.

Scarface fell dead to the ground. Brand jerked and twisted his sword free. The others had a moment to attack him during this vulnerability, but they did not move. Shock marked their faces.

Brand looked down at the man he had killed. He had not wanted to do it, but he would not have the deaths of innocent travelers on his conscience. Better the death of a murderer.

Brand glanced at Kareste. She was still mounted, but her sword was drawn, and it dripped blood. A man lay beneath it, dead also, his limp hand open near the great diamond.

Kareste dismounted. She stepped over the body and picked up the jewel. For a moment she studied it, and then she tossed it to Brand.

He caught it. And his movement frightened the bandits that still stood, and they fled, hurrying downriver.

"You're full of surprises," Kareste said. "And just when I thought I was getting to know you." Her eyes glittered as she studied him, but Brand could not read her expression.

"Time to go," he said.

They mounted and rode into the shallow water of the ford. Behind them several men staggered up, but they seemed frozen in place by awe, and they made no move to follow.

The horses splashed through the water, and it frothed and foamed about their legs. After a while they clambered up onto the little island in the middle of the river, and then plunged into the water again.

Eventually, they made the far bank. The road started once more, a smooth and wide surface, turfed and slightly sloped to run water from the center to the sides.

They trotted forward. Brand studied the land ahead, and then the sky. He saw nothing to alarm him. Even the hawk was gone.

As they rode he sensed Kareste's eyes on him. Probably, she guessed why he had not killed the men and what he was trying to do.

"You can fight," she said eventually. "That much I already knew, but you still managed to surprise me anyway."

Brand shrugged. Most of the people who knew how well he could fight were dead.

Kareste did not take her eyes off him. "But you should have killed them – killed them all. I would have."

Brand did not answer. He rode slightly ahead, and he felt her eyes burning into his back.

18. Hope for the Hopeless

"Come!" commanded Carnhaina, and Arell felt the force of her will. It lashed her like a whip, so strong was it, yet it was not even directed at her.

Arell tore her eyes away from the queen. Her concern was for her patient. Aranloth remained still, yet to her expert gaze he looked different. There was more color in his skin, at least as best as she could tell by the shifting lights of torch and star. But more than that, she saw the rise and fall of his chest as he breathed: faster, deeper, more lifelike than before.

"Come!" commanded Carnhaina, and the spirit of Aranloth heard her call and followed her voice. Suddenly, he tensed where he lay on the stretcher; the blood seeped anew from the two wounds on his chest, and his eyes flicked open, wild, uncertain, unknowing of where he was or how he got there.

Arell knelt down and put her hand to his hot brow. She soothed him, and though she saw that he was back from the near-dead, she saw also that he was weak, terribly weak.

She spared a quick glance at Carnhaina, but the queen was already fading. The arm that held the spear seemed insubstantial as it slowly fell. Her eyes were closed. The starlight seemed dim and the torches gutted. In the flickering air the motes of dust that had formed her figure drifted apart and settled slowly into the sarcophagus once more.

The great queen was gone, but Aranloth was back. And yet, a voice, imperious and commanding as always, rang out as though the very stone atop the tower spoke:

Aranloth is returned, but the hope of Cardoroth, as always it has done, rests with Brand. Remember!

Gilhain surveyed the enemy. From the rampart that had withstood the seething masses of darkness, he looked out into a bright morning.

The enemy remained. Fear remained. The knowledge of likely defeat remained. And yet there was hope too. For Aranloth, pale and sickly, yet alive, stood near him. Or rather, he leaned against the stone of the battlement in view of the enemy.

Aranloth had placed himself there. Without speaking he had come with the dawn. What his thoughts were, Gilhain did not know, but he knew this much at least; even in his weakened state the lòhren's mind was still sharp. The enemy would see him, and whatever spies the enemy had, whatever means of gathering news that they relied on, they would have heard of his collapse and hoped for his death. When the sun had come up, they had all seen that their hope was cheated.

Gilhain moved to stand beside him. "He's still out there, somewhere," he said.

Aranloth knew that he meant Brand. The lòhren's tired eyes looked into his own.

"Do you fear that he has betrayed Cardoroth? That he has betrayed our trust in him?"

Gilhain slowly shook his head. "No, I don't believe that. But I can't help but wonder what he's doing and what he's thinking. If what Carnhaina said is true, and Arell must have told you of it, he recovered the second half of Shurilgar's staff, and he escaped the tombs of the Letharn. Yet the staff is not destroyed, and Cardoroth is sorely pressed. What if the sorcerers commence another attack? You're very frail, my old friend."

Aranloth looked anxious. "There are many chances in the world, for good or for ill. Something has happened. More is going on than we know, and I wish I knew what it was. But I know this much at least. I trust Brand, and I gave him my staff, and I gave him my diadem. Those things are symbols, but with my trust in him I gave him power also, the power embodied by those symbols. He now represents the lòhrens, and he must make choices even as a lòhren, and the fate of Alithoras has become his concern, not just Cardoroth, no matter how much he loves us."

Gilhain thought about that. There was evidently more going on than he knew. He had thought that lending Brand the staff and diadem was just a practical means of giving him some power to fight off enemies. It appeared to be more than that though, but in just what way he could not quite see.

Aurellin joined their conversation. "Brand is not as others," she said. "Whatever he does, he does for us, and perhaps now also for others too. But I will continue to trust in him, to hope in him, as I have done before."

Her words struck a chord with Gilhain. That was how he felt, even though after what Carnhaina had said, he should have been riddled with doubt.

Lornach interrupted his musings. "Look over there," the Durlin said.

Gilhain followed his gaze. He saw nothing at first, but taking his eyes off the closer northward fields and looking in the distance, he saw what the sharp eyes of the little man had noticed before anyone else: a dust cloud.

They watched in silence. Soon other men along the wall noticed it too, but there was nothing anyone could do but wait and continue to watch. That it was caused by riders was obvious, and a great many of them too, but who they were and what they were doing was beyond any guess.

The cloud deepened. The riders drew closer, and there was an occasional flash of metal and color. As they approached, Gilhain estimated their numbers. He took it to be a large group, perhaps a thousand strong.

"Is it an attack on the enemy?" Lornach asked. "Or reinforcements for them?"

Gilhain was beginning to understand. "No," he answered. "It's not either of those things. Most especially, it's not an attack. Look at the horde. They have set up no defense, moved no troops to face the riders."

"Then what is it?" Lornach asked. "And what difference can a mere thousand riders make?"

Gilhain did not answer. Nor did Aranloth speak, though by the look on his face he had guessed the same answer that Gilhain knew in his heart.

"It depends on who leads them," Aurellin said.

Lornach pulled at an earlobe, trying to figure it out. While he thought, the column drew closer.

"They're not Azan," he said. "Nor are the horses the alar breed of the south. These are northerners, that much is now obvious. But if not Azan, then who?"

They continued to watch. The elug war drums muttered away, sending a different message from normal; it was not a battle beat. And this was proven as the horde opened its ranks and allowed the column through.

The men on the walls were watching also, and this made them uneasy. It was bad enough that the enemy received reinforcements, however small the number in the greater scheme of things, but it was worse that they were men, and northerners also. It was not something that they could comprehend.

There was much movement in the camp below. Messengers were sent, riders went back and forth, and the horde itself was excited by some news that rippled through it.

"We could have done without this," Gilhain said.

Lornach shrugged. "It's still only a thousand odd men."

"But look at the horde. They have news to consider, something different to think about, and likely enough a reason for better hope. All those things are taking their minds off their recent defeats sooner than would otherwise have happened. The timing is bad for us." Gilhain straightened his shoulders as though mentally preparing himself for something yet to come. "But it is what it is, and we'll deal with it as we've dealt with everything else."

A little while later a small group of riders emerged from the ranks of the enemy. They wore bright colors, and the harness of their horses glittered. They were proud men, sitting astride their mounts as though they owned the very land and all that they could see.

At the head of the group rode one man, aloof and prouder even than his companions. On his head he wore a winged helm, a Halathrin helm, for no others gleamed as did they, or bore the mark of such craftsmanship. But Cardoroth had seen its like before. It seemed to some that it was Brand returned, but others said nay. Brand's helm was horned.

The man's mail coat shimmered in the light. No cheap thing was it either, and there were few in the realm who wore armor to match it. Likewise, his sword was a precious thing. Light flashed from the diamonds and precious stones set at its pommel. Yet he bore the look of a man who could fight, and the sword was not just for ceremony.

They approached, proud and haughty. No flag of truce they raised, deeming it beneath them, yet no arrow sped from bow nor jeering word from mouth to rebuke them.

Just behind the lead rider was a second man. His face was pockmarked, his long black hair held bound by a thick ring of beaten gold. And he carried a staff with a banner wrapped around it.

They came to a stop near the wall. The lead rider did not turn, but he made a flicking gesture to the man immediately behind him. The rider undid a leather thong that held the banner wrapped tight in its position. When it was untied, he held high the staff and shook free the cloth.

All the men along the Cardurleth saw it. The Durlin saw it, and Lornach saw it and finally understood. It was a well-known banner: on a sable background was threaded a gold eagle, one taloned claw lifted and raking at an invisible enemy, its great wings half stretched out.

"The royal banner!" hissed Lornach, and he looked sharply at the king.

"Indeed," Gilhain said. "None should dare to unfurl it except at my order, and none do – except one."

"Hvargil," muttered the queen.

Gilhain had been ready for this. He knew it would come one day, guessed even when he first saw the column of riders who it was that led them. But it was still a shock, not that he should be any longer shocked at what his younger half-brother did. It was not the first time that he had consorted with the enemy. His capacity for treachery knew no equal, unless it was the extent of his lust for the throne of Cardoroth.

Hvargil reached up slowly and removed his helm, tucking it under his arm in a gesture that reminded Gilhain of their father. The horse seemed restless beneath him, but with a squeeze of his legs he guided it a few steps forward. The other riders stayed where they were.

"Hail, half-brother, and well met," Hvargil called.

Gilhain raised an eyebrow. "Hail, brother. But our meeting would perhaps have been better if you brought better company."

Hvargil glanced back at the elug host and shrugged. "A means to an end," he replied.

"Exactly," Gilhain answered. "But which of you is the means and which the end?"

Hvargil laughed. "You're very witty for a man who knows the answer to your own question. The only end we need speak of is your reign over Cardoroth. It draws to a conclusion soon. And your life with it."

"Perhaps," Gilhain answered. "Certainly, we're outnumbered. But then again, things started off that way, and yet we're still here. If I were a betting man, I'd stake all I owned on it staying that way. Why don't you change sides, while you still can?"

The horse beneath his brother moved restlessly, but Hvargil betrayed no sign of nerves.

"Oh, I don't think so. I grant you this, you've held on well, I'll not deny it. But we both know that time will wear you down. I've made the right bet, and I'll stick with it."

Gilhain shrugged. "It's your head. As I recall, you made the same bet on a battlefield not so long ago. And against the odds Cardoroth won, despite your treachery."

Hvargil showed a flicker of displeasure, but he covered it swiftly.

"You were lucky that day. Ninety nine times out of a hundred you would have lost."

Gilhain smiled. "I'm a lucky king."

"And I'll be a long reigning one."

"Is that what they promised you? Do you really think they'll just give you the crown if the city falls and leave you to play kings and queens by yourself?"

"What a way with words you have. But actions speak louder than words. Consider this." He drew his sword and held the helm up high in the other hand. "You know what these are. They're Halathrin forged. The helm alone is worth more than any crown in any kingdom of men. And the sword is priceless. These they have given me in token of riches to come. And they *will* come, for the leader of this host rewards well those who serve him loyally."

The sword and helm glittered and sparkled. Gilhain knew their worth, and their rarity.

"I've seen their like before. But the man who bore them impressed me more than any such possessions. You can dress a pony up with ribbons, but you can't turn it into a warhorse."

"More words of wisdom. But where is your precious Brand now? Alive? Dead? Fled back into the wild lands from whence he came?"

Gilhain did not answer straight away. The first option was his hope, the last his fear. But Aranloth spoke for the first time.

"You know where Brand has gone, and what his quest is. Your elùgroth masters will have revealed that to you, at least if you're as high in their confidence as you think. But I grow bored of this banter. Speak your message, for surely they put one in your mouth, and then return to them."

"Bored?" Hvargil said. "You've come back from near death only to be bored the next day? Perhaps you should have considered staying dead." He placed the helm back on his head and sheathed the sword. "You see, old man, I'm very well informed indeed."

135

"But still you don't name Brand's quest, for I know elùgroths better than you, and they will not have told you of their fear."

Hvargil gripped tight his horse's reins. "The elùgroths fear *nothing*."

"How little you know them," Aranloth said. "But speak. Deliver your message and begone."

Hvargil seemed supremely confident. He did not speak to Gilhain or Aranloth, but rather to the men atop the wall, knowing that those who could not hear his words would hear them second hand soon enough.

"I know your numbers – the living and the wounded and the dead. I know where your food is stockpiled, and how much is left, and I know which wells in the city have run dry and which still supply good water. I know that Aranloth was healed last night by the spirit of Carnhaina, she who once ruled this realm but now is dead."

He paused for a moment, the hover of a smile on his mouth.

"That came as a surprise. The elùgroths did not like it, but the world turns in strange ways, and many things happen beyond the ken of mortal men. So indeed Aranloth taught me himself when I was a young lad, only as high as his knee and fascinated by the stories he used to tell. But that was long ago, and times change, for cities as much as for men. Carnhaina was a great queen, but her time is long since passed. These are our days now. It's our turn to shine and grow and flourish beneath the sun. It's now time to befriend the south, to help each other, to put an end to the long years of strife and war and fear. We can make that happen. Can you see it? Can your mind encompass how good it would be? The truth is, if you follow Gilhain, you will die. If you follow me, you will live to see the future you just pictured. Follow me, and prosper! That is your choice. Put down your weapons. Put aside the stories you have heard of the south. They're lies. Come! Join me, and put an end to fear and the shadow of death. Come now, what do you say?"

Hvargil ceased speaking. He looked up at the Cardurleth, his gaze serene, his posture confident. He looked every bit a king, and a glorious king at that, and the royal banner fluttered proudly beside him.

There was a stir all along the wall. Gilhain remained as he was. He did not answer Hvargil himself. To speak now was to try to take the choice away from the men, and that would be a mistake. He could almost see Hvargil's chagrin that he avoided that trap. And yet, all along the wall, men spoke to one another. A ripple ran through them, for hope to the hopeless was a powerful gift.

19. The Great North Road

For the next two days Brand and Kareste rode at a fast pace. And they found that the Great North Road was good for riding. It may have been built in ancient times when the Halathrin dwelled in the north of the land as well as their more southerly forest realm of Halathar, but when the immortals built something, it lasted. The turf was green and springy, the path straight, and the gentle slope to left and right from the middle ensured the ground was never wet.

Brand knew there was danger in staying on the road. It was in the open. It was a place that may be watched. And it was a place where any of their enemies would know exactly where they came from, where they were going and how long it would take them to get there. But the speed it enabled was a necessity.

The two days of hard riding had seen them travel far though, and for the moment, in safety. And having done that, they could now veer away from the road and head west. Lòrenta lay in that direction, and the final destination of their quest. The Halathrin that had been trapped in the form of beasts roamed those hills, and when they reached them, well, Brand did not like to think too far ahead.

The riding was harder now. It was still grassland, but there were many obstacles in the form of rough ground, little creeks and gullies, and an increasing feeling of riding uphill.

Lòrenta was close. The hills themselves were visible, wild and gorse covered. And even in the middle of the day many were capped by cloud or fog.

They spoke little as they travelled. Kareste wrestled with something in her own mind, and it seemed at times that she had nearly forgotten that he was there. The days of peace and comradeship that he had enjoyed were gone, and he wondered if he would ever feel their like again.

Another two days passed. The weather was cold and overcast, but it did not rain. Ever they climbed upward, and though the river was now to their west, the ground oftentimes became boggy. Between that, and the upward slope, their speed reduced greatly.

"We're in the foothills now," Kareste said. "We must be prepared, for the Halathrin become beasts may roam this far."

It was more than Kareste had said all day, and Brand took the opportunity to ask a question. He wanted to know more about what they faced.

"What should I expect of these creatures?" he asked. "And if necessity demands it, how best can they be fought?"

She did not look at him as she answered, her gaze roving the lands ahead of them as they rode, but at least she did answer, even if her voice was quiet and her manner brusque.

"There are about twenty of them. They're strong. And they're fast, being in the shape of wolves, though bigger."

"So they're much like the sendings that the elùgroths set on my trail near Cardoroth?"

She shook her head. "Not really. They might look similar at a distance, but they're near impossible to kill. These are Halathrin changed by sorcery. They're strong, fast, intelligent and graceful beyond any wild animal. Almost you can see the Halathrin that is in them, and the

Halathrin are immortal. These creatures would be hard to kill, and no lòhren would *want* to knowing who was trapped inside the sorcerous form that shaped them. The elùgroths knew what they were doing when they conceived their plan."

"But why create them at all? What's their purpose, for surely the lòhrens are safe within the walls of their keep."

"Their purpose is to hinder the lòhrens from coming and going. They would not try to kill the beasts, even if they could, for they would kill the Halathrin inside them. And they have no way to reverse the sorcery, as do I with Shurilgar's staff. But more than that, I think they did it out of spite. The elùgroths have no greater enemy than lòhrens and, at least in the past, the Halathrin. To subject them both to this abomination, one to endure it, one to see it, would be a satisfaction to them."

"How did the elùgroths achieve it? The Halathrin are mighty warriors, and it's said that even their warriors have skill with magic."

"The Halathrin band pursued the elùgroths after they stole the half of Shurilgar's staff that they guarded. It may be that they were deliberately allowed to do so, to lure them away from their home and toward Lòrenta. It may be that the elùgroths conceived of that part of the plan from the beginning. Yet one way or the other, they were led into these hills. Khamdar made sure of that."

"But if Khamdar went to Cardoroth from here after transforming the Halathrin, they had the staff right from the start of the siege?"

"Of course."

"Then why didn't they use it from the beginning?"

"I think they held it in reserve. Perhaps they wished to study it more before they used it. It cannot be used without effects, that much is certain, and they will have discovered so after they used it first in Lòrenta."

Brand wondered what effect it would have on her, but he did not raise that point.

"How do you know all this?" he asked.

"Because I was there. It wasn't that far from where we are now. The elùgroths came through with the Halathrin pursuit close behind. I followed, and I saw things that I wish I had not."

"Why were you even here in the first place? The lòhrens suspended you from their order."

She shrugged. "Maybe I yearned for what I didn't have. I don't know. The hills of Lòrenta have a way of getting under your skin, and this place is home to me. It looks desolate, but there are many beauties here for those with the eyes to see them."

He did not press her on the point. In truth, he did not have to. He knew better than most what it was like to lose a home, and to yearn for it.

He glanced around. The hills marched away from him, rising higher and expanding. They *were* desolate, covered in dried grasses and gorse, wreathed in mists and barren of farms, livestock and cultivation. Lòrenta was a wild and remote place, a place of great loneliness. But he thought he might like it too if he explored it.

The damp path they followed curved around a small stand of white-barked birches. It was the first stand of many, for it seemed nearly the only tree that grew on or near the hills.

"What now?" he asked.

"What else?" she replied. "We find the beasts – or they find us first. That's much more likely. And then I try to reverse the spell the elùgroths used. It won't be easy, even with the other half of Shurilgar's staff."

"Can you do it?"

"You have a lot of questions today, don't you?"

141

"Answering a question with a question of your own isn't much of an answer," he said with a tight grin.

"If I had a better reply, I would've offered you that instead."

20. By Ancient Right

Hvargil's words hung in the air. Gilhain remained silent. Yet after a while a soldier gave his own answer. He did not yell, but his slow reply was loud enough to be heard by many. And there was an emotion in his voice that made men listen.

"I lost friends the day you betrayed us on the battlefield, Hvargil. I'll not bow to you."

There was silence again, but another soldier spoke into it from further along the wall.

"I lost a brother that day," he said. "When he was younger I taught him how to use a sword. It didn't protect him from an elug arrow in the neck, though. If not for your treachery, the enemy might have been defeated before that arrow was ever shot." He paused, and then added. "I'll not bow to you, either."

A third soldier called out, his voice ragged and harsh. "I lost five of my friends that day. Men that I grew up with. Men that I knew all my life. They didn't have to die. They'd still be here if not for you, so as far as I'm concerned I'd rather bury you upside down in a cesspit than bow to you."

The men seemed suddenly unleashed. They jeered by the hundreds, and then by the thousands. One voice rose above them all. "Half-brother, and half-wit!"

This caused a ripple of laughter, and the chant was taken up and cast into Hvargil's teeth.

Gilhain suppressed a smile. He had never had any reason to worry. But the vehemence of the men's reaction surprised him. It must also have surprised Hvargil, but he endured it unflinching and with no hint of his feelings showing.

The chant eventually died away and Gilhain spoke at last.

"You have your answer, Hvargil. Now go."

"Not just yet, Gilhain."

Hvargil drew himself up. He looked proud, every inch a king, and there was something to admire in the strength of his will, for to look like that after the jeering of the soldiers was more than most could manage.

"I have an answer to one question," he said. "So be it. A king does not rule by the will of the people, he takes the people and bends them to his own. That you will all learn, at least those who live. But this is my second question." He turned directly to Gilhain and looked up at him with an expressionless face. "Will you honor the customs of our ancestors?"

Gilhain felt a shadow of fear at those words. The question was not idle, but he could not see its purpose, and that worried him.

"What customs?" he asked.

"That is a poor answer. Either you do, or you do not. But I'll make it easy for you to reply, for by your answer the people shall know you." He gazed once more along the Cardurleth, seeming to make eye contact with all who stood there. "We are of the Camar. We trace our heritage back to long before Cardoroth was even founded. Our ways, our customs, our rights are ancient. There once was a right of challenge for the kingship of our people, a right of challenge by combat. It ensured that no weakling, and no coward, ever sat on the throne. That law still exists, and I invoke it."

Things made sense to Gilhain now, but this was tricky ground, and he must answer carefully.

"Maybe," he said. "But it has not been invoked in the history of Cardoroth. If ever it was used, it goes back to a time before we lived in cities. It may have been invoked then, if legends can be believed, but things have changed since then. So what if you won the kingship that way? I'm an older man by far than you. Beating me in combat would prove only that you're younger. It would not make you a better king nor make the people accept you. It would achieve nothing."

Hvargil looked at him smugly. "And yet it is my right. Will you deny it?"

Gilhain thought hard. There was a trap in this, and Aranloth leaned slightly toward him and spoke softly.

"Beware," the lòhren said.

"What does he hope to achieve?" Gilhain asked quietly.

"Not the kingship, for as you say the people would not accept him. I think you can take this at face value. He wants to kill you, either in combat or through foul means. That would be a great blow to the morale of our defense. I cannot guarantee your safety from sorcery if you accept the challenge and go out into the field."

Gilhain considered that. "But if I don't accept, that will undermine morale."

"So it would, and certainly the enemy always tries to paint us as cowards, but it would not impact morale as much. No one would really expect you to fight him. There's a twenty year age difference."

For the first time in a long while Gilhain wished he were young again. He had accepted old age, but at times like this his mind wanted to make promises his body could not keep.

"I don't like to suggest this," Gilhain whispered. "But there might be another option beside accept or decline.

145

I'm an old man – under the ancient customs that Hvargil's invoking I'm allowed a champion to fight for me."

"That's true, but whoever you chose as champion would face the same dangers, and there would still be a loss of morale if he was beaten."

"But to refuse is to allow them an uncontested victory, and they would try to build on it. It's morale that holds this defense together, as much as, perhaps even more so, than swords."

To that, Aranloth gave a slight nod, but he did not answer.

Gilhain straightened, but what he was going to say to Hvargil was forestalled.

"I'll do it," Lornach offered. The Durlin was close by, although Gilhain had not thought him close enough to hear what was said.

"I'll do it, and I'll do it gladly. I lost friends on that same battlefield the other soldiers mentioned. I have my own grudge against your brother."

Gilhain looked at him earnestly. Brand knew how to choose his men, for the Durlin were loyal even beyond the normal for handpicked troops.

"I need you to guard me," Gilhain answered.

Lornach shook his head. "Even as Brand is still guarding you, albeit in a different way through pursuing his quest, so too must I. I'm short, but I can fight. And if it comes to it, it would not be the first time that I've faced sorcery. I feel it in my bones – I was born for this fight."

Gilhain bit his lip. It was not like him to be indecisive, and he became aware that all the men on the wall now waited on whatever answer he would give to the challenge.

"What do you think, Aranloth?"

The lòhren did not answer. Instead, his eyes seemed to gaze into the distance as though he was trying to peer into the shadow-shrouded future. What he saw there, if

146

anything at all, Gilhain did not know. Aranloth gave no sign.

And yet, within the space of a handful of heartbeats the lòhren looked back at him sharply.

21. Impending Doom

Aranloth spoke. "I cannot see the future. I'm weak, and foresight comes and goes to rhythms of its own. The choice, O king, is a hard one. I discern the potential for great harm, but also the chance of great good. It hangs in the balance."

Gilhain thought about that for a moment and then raised an eyebrow.

"They say a lòhren's advice can be two edged. Now I know what they mean."

"Advice is a serious business, my King. It's easy to give, but harder to get right." The old man sighed. "But since you press me, I'll add this. I cannot foresee the outcome of a fight between Lornach and Hvargil, and without that I can offer nothing that you don't already know. And yet, Brand chose the Durlin. He chose all of them, and whatever twist of fate made him who and what he is, made him someone to whom you would entrust the fate of the kingdom, may well also touch those he chose to surround himself with. Luck gathers luck unto itself."

Gilhain considered that. He was not sure if it added anything to the lòhren's previous comment, but time to decide ran out on him.

"Gilhain!" his half-brother called. "Enough of this! Will you gossip and talk all day like an old washerwoman with her cronies? Fate waits for no man. Decide, and be done with it!"

Gilhain grinned at him "I'm in no hurry, Hvargil. There's nowhere pressing I have to go, and fate, like death, comes when you least expect it. So you will discover when you're older – if fate is kinder to you than you deserve. But as it happens, I've made my choice."

Shorty wore the white surcoat and armor of the Durlin. He looked resplendent, as they all did in the uniform. But he did not feel like it, nor did he care to be. They all insisted on calling him Lornach now, even Brand when they were not alone, but he had been Shorty all his life, and there was an attitude that went with his true self even if it did not match his true name. He did not give a damn for wealth or position or influence. What excited him was adventure, and that was something that he felt now. Adventure, risk and exhilaration all coursed through his veins. He felt alive.

He was outside the Arach Neben, the west gate of the Cardurleth. The steel emblem that decorated it, the representation of the Morning Star, was the last thing that he saw before he turned to face the horde. The entire mass of the enemy, and the single man that for just a moment embodied it – Hvargil, was before him.

Nothing stood between him and the great mass of foes who would like to tear him to pieces, and never had he felt more alive.

But they would not tear him to pieces. At least not just yet. And he would do his best to ensure that Hvargil did not either, for the king had agreed to make him his champion, and he therefore represented, at least for a little while, the entire city of Cardoroth.

He felt *alive*, and he intended to stay that way.

The Durlin never wore any special ornament or insignia, but for this occasion Aranloth had tied about his waist a cloth belt in the colors of the king, and the Eagle of Cardoroth was blazoned upon it. It felt strange to wear it, for none but the king were allowed to bear that emblem on their person, and even Aranloth, who had watched him all the while with tired eyes, had given him a strange look at the end.

Hvargil strode to meet him. The small band that had come with the traitor to the wall withdrew. The two men faced each other between the city wall and the dark mass of the elug horde.

"You?" the man who would rule Cardoroth said. "You're the king's champion? Why don't you come back when you're full grown?"

Shorty grinned at him. "I'm short, *my King*, he said sarcastically, but I'm not stupid. You're trying to upset me so that I fight rashly, and that means that you're scared. And well should you be, for you know nothing of me, but I know all about you."

"Well, I know this much. You've learned a few Durlin tricks, for just now you're trying to insinuate doubt into my mind. But enough of these games. Let our blades speak."

Hvargil donned his helm that he had carried under his arm. It looked to Shorty much like Brand's, only it was perhaps more beautiful, for the wings on it flicked back like a graceful hawk in flight. But the horns on Brand's spoke of mad battle and a will of adamantine determination that would never falter.

And then Hvargil drew his sword with a flourish. It nearly seemed to leap from the sheath of its own accord, and the pattern-welded blade shimmered and caught the light from jewels and precious stones on the hilt and threw it into the air like a mist of light. Shorty had a sudden sense of what it would be like to face Brand in battle, and it was not a good feeling.

But it was not Brand before him. It was an enemy. An enemy of Cardoroth, and someone that Shorty despised. He held his own grudge against this man, and he would

150

now seek to repay him for past treachery. Justice called for no less.

And he who stood before him did not have Brand's quiet but strong presence. Nor was the sword the same. Brand's was plainer, for this was covered in strange runes of victory. Shorty had seen their like before, though he could not remember where. But he realized that the runes were an addition made well after the sword's ancient forging, and probably ordered by Hvargil himself. No, he was not like Brand at all.

Shorty donned his own helm. It was unadorned, but of good quality. Yet no helm would protect him from a full-blooded blow of a Halathrin blade. Skill alone would see him through this situation, if anything could, and not armor.

He drew his sword. It did not ring as it came from the sheath. It did not glitter as though cold flame burned inside it. It was not pattern-welded nor marked by runes of power. Yet it was well made, and he kept it sharp. And though it had none of the long history of a Halathrin blade that was forged before the Camar migrated west, it had a history for *him*, for he had used it since he was little more than a boy, and before that it had belonged to his father. There were thousands like it in the city, but it was *his*, and he knew the feel of it in his hands with surpassing familiarity.

Hvargil gave the customary bow before a duel. He bent at the waist, but not low, and the point of his sword touched the ground. That was an insult, and though Shorty was not of the nobility he knew it. A dirty blade was more likely to lead to infection, and it was a mark of disrespect.

Shorty gave his own bow. He kept the point of his sword low, but it did not touch the ground. He bowed his head also, as was the custom. But he dropped it a little lower than he was supposed to, and he squeezed his eyes into slits.

Hvargil did not surprise him. The man-who-would-be-king straightened and flicked dirt up and into Shorty's face. It was intended to blind him, and so it might have if not for his precautions.

Shorty kept his head low and sunk into a fighting crouch. The dirt flew about his face and some pebbles rang against his helm, but it did not affect him.

Hvargil was poised to attack, but he saw that his trick was of no avail and did not move in.

"A low ploy," Shorty said. "But further proof that you're scared. If you really believed in your superiority you wouldn't bother with the like."

Hvargil grunted. "And nor would you with your continued, but nevertheless futile, efforts to seed doubt into my mind."

They began to circle each other. Hvargil moved with grace and balance. Shorty stayed lower and moved less.

Hvargil struck the first blow. His blade flicked out, and it was met by Shorty's. Steel on steel rang through the air like the one-off peal of a small bell. And then they separated once more. It was nothing more than a first test, and yet they both learned much from that single touch.

Shorty knew Hvargil had a reputation as a great fighter. Yet still a shiver of fear ran through him. He now knew that reputation was well founded, for his opponent was incredibly quick and also strong. It was not a common combination. And to make matters worse, Hvargil had the greater reach. Yet Shorty was used to fighting taller men, and he had his ways to deal with that. He began to wonder if they would be enough though.

Gilhain leaned on the battlement, his hands gripping tight the stone. "Lornach is outmatched," he whispered.

152

Taingern answered him. "That man has been outmatched all his life, but he's still alive. His is a heart that does not give up."

Aranloth did not speak, and Gilhain turned to him for an opinion.

"What do you think?"

A long while the lòhren took to answer and it seemed as though a great weariness was on him, or perhaps he was in some sort of trance. But at length he replied.

"I do not see what you see. I perceive from afar the elùgroths. They sit together, their minds bent upon the battle. They are near the elug war drums. Those drums beat. Sorcery joins the sound, twines with it, yet it is subtle and I do not see its purpose. I see Hvargil, full of pride, but also of doubt. He has cast all he has in a desperate gamble by joining the elùgroths and making this challenge. He is desperate and deadly dangerous. Lornach is fearful. But he knows in his bones that live or die this fight buys time, if nothing else. It buys time for Brand, and every hour that we survive is another hour in which Brand may yet prevail. And he senses something else. He senses it in the air, even as do I. *Sorcery*."

Shorty felt sweat run down his back. His arms ached and his wrists were sore. But he was untouched by his opponent's blade. And yet Hvargil was also untouched. They circled and fought and delivered blows and retreated. All to no advantage. Not yet. But it could not go on like this. One of them must soon land a blow.

His hands were clammy. He had a sense of impending doom, and that was not like him at all. But he fought on, the sound of steel on steel ringing through the air and the thrum of the blows running up his arm.

Suddenly, he saw a gap in Hvargil's defense. He made to strike, but even as his weight shifted he heard the war drums of the elugs change beat and it seemed as though the very earth beneath his feet buckled.

Instead of striking a blow he staggered sideways, struggling to keep upright. Hvargil had no such problem. His eyes gleamed within the shadow of the helm and he seized his opportunity to attack.

The Halathrin blade darted like a tongue of lightening. Shorty saw it come. He tried to withdraw, but he merely stumbled further, and yet it was that which saved him. For instead of taking the blow to his neck, the glittering edge missed that death mark. Yet still it caught him a glancing blow on the arm.

He leapt back. The sword fell from his grip, and red blood dripped down his fingers. Pain stung him, sharp and deep.

Shorty stepped further away from his opponent. He drew his knife, but he knew that he was a dead man. Not from his wounded arm: that would need many stitches, but from lack of a real weapon. Hvargil stood between him and his sword, and the sword was his only chance at life.

There was only one thing that he could try. He must somehow distract his opponent and retrieve his weapon. But Hvargil looked at him with cold, unblinking eyes. He was not a man to give such chances, and he stalked forward now, confident and poised.

Shorty saw no reason to draw things out. He flung the last weapon he had. The knife spun through the air. It was no defense against a sword, but in this way he might be able to use it to throw his opponent off balance for just long enough to get passed him and reach his blade.

Hvargil saw the blade coming. Whether his reflexes were excellent, or he guessed the move in advance, Shorty did not know. But his enemy merely lowered his head and the knife struck sparks off the helm and clattered away.

Hvargil barely moved, and there was not one chance in a thousand of getting past him. Shorty did not even try.

"Ready to die, little man?" Hvargil asked.

Aranloth stiffened. "Too late I understand the foul sorcery," he said.

"Can you help him with lòhrengai?" Gilhain asked.

"No," the lòhren answered. "It takes time to do something like what the sorcerers did, and anything more obvious would only work against us in the end. Lornach is on his own."

"Then he is doomed," Gilhain said. "A weaponless man cannot beat the likes of Hvargil."

Taingern, standing close but not taking his eyes off the battle, spoke.

"A Durlin is never weaponless," he said.

Shorty looked for some sort of an opening, for anything. But Hvargil gave him nothing. Worse, he had decided out of spite to move backward and pick up Shorty's own sword. That was his best opportunity to attack, but Hvargil was waiting for him to do it. Shorty could feel his expectation, and let the moment pass because of it.

Hvargil flung the blade far behind him. Shorty had the strange feeling that he would never again hold the familiar hilt in his hand, the same hilt that his father had gripped. A slow anger began to burn inside him.

Hvargil advanced. Shorty retreated. It occurred to him that he could run back to the gate, but that was not in him. He could also beg for mercy, but that was not in him either. Nor did he think it would be granted. Hvargil did not understand the concept of mercy.

Shorty took some deep breaths. He was thinking the wrong way, and he knew it. He must accept his death, if so it must be, but he would not die without one last attempt, no matter how desperate the plan seemed, to win this fight.

22. We Hunt

Brand and Kareste did not have to seek the beasts that the twisted sorcery of Khamdar had unleashed upon the world. The Halathrin transformed into beasts found them.

The two travelers had entered the foothills of Lòrenta. Those hills now climbed about them, but where Brand and Kareste rode along low paths between rocky ledges and creeks, following some ancient trail, the ground was damp, or more often even boggy.

As they penetrated deeper into the wild lands of hill and moor, the temperature dropped and thick fogs clung to the earth like a blanket thrown over a bed.

But the fog was not warm and comforting; it hung cold and clammy in the air, making it hard to see or to hear. And it hid things. Creatures roamed unseen, but the evidence of their existence was left in the moist earth the next morning, for the trail was marked ahead of them as well as behind them. Brand was no tracker, and he did not know how to read the signs, but something was drawn to them, though he did not think it was the beasts. If so, he guessed they would have attacked.

They moved now up and along the ridges, sometimes dropping back into dark hollows before the trail took them high again, but up or down they ever moved toward the center of the hills.

The silence of the wild land grew about them, and there was little to be seen in grass or sky or tree. Yet Brand knew there was wildlife here, he just did not have the skill or knowledge to observe it. Yet for all its remoteness, it was the kind of place that he would love to explore.

They camped one night beside a tarn. The dark water was still, so still as to seem as glass. Weeping willows grew about it, their drooping branches and long leaves overhanging the shadowy water.

In the trees were crows. The birds flapped near silently, stretching their wings and cawing in subdued fashion. They croaked and called and squawked, but the noise they made was quiet, or else the moisture-laden air deadened it.

All through the night the birds muttered to themselves, and no other sound was to be heard in all the world.

The next morning dawned, but the sun was little more than a white haze in the fog-shrouded east. The crows stayed where they were, and they became still and silent, looking about them with tilted heads and beady eyes.

Brand and Kareste ate a cold breakfast. They could find no dry timber for a fire.

Kareste was anxious, her green-gold eyes studying their surrounds. At length, she stood.

"Something comes," she whispered.

Brand stood also, his restless hand fondling his sword hilt.

"What is it?"

She concentrated. Her fingers twitched absently on the broken half of Shurilgar's staff.

"The sorcery that I must undo. My greatest test."

Brand felt a chill run through his bones. *No. Not your greatest test. But that will follow swiftly after.*

He heard nothing except the slow drip of moisture from the long willow leaves. And then, ever so faintly, he heard the padding of paws along dark trails somewhere in the nearby birch wood. The fog seemed to grow heavier. The white haze of the sun darkened.

"They bring it with them," Kareste whispered.

"The fog? How is that possible? They're now only beasts."

"They are what I told you earlier – creatures from the otherworld. They have their own powers, but they are bound to this earth not by men or elugs, but by the immortal Halathrin. That strengthens them, makes them different from anything you have seen before. They have powers of body and mind, and some of magic, as you would call it. Expect nothing of them. Be prepared for anything.

Brand was not sure what to make of her words, except that he did not like them.

Not long after, the creatures came into view. They were shy, but they made no real attempt to stay concealed. Kareste had been right about them: they were not like the hounds that had pursued him near Lake Alithorin. These beasts, although large and muscular, had no tufted fur or bare patches of skin. They were long limbed and sleek, and their coats were a glorious white, bright as the full moon.

There was fog all through the hills, but these creatures certainly did seem to bring their own with them. Wherever they paced, a silvery shimmer fell about them. They were sleek, graceful, beautiful. And they were otherworldly. That much he could see at a glance.

The beasts padded closer, their long legs delicately covering the ground, their paws sure footed. They seemed as dancers, their movements more fluid and natural than anything he had ever seen, and yet their every movement had a purpose. Not only did they draw closer, but they spread out and formed a half-moon ring about the two travelers.

Brand and Kareste backed away toward the picketed horses near the edge of the tarn. When the first wolf growled, it sent a shiver up his spine. For all the grace and beauty of the beast, the sound that came from it was hideous, all the worse for being unexpected. Its fangs were long and sharp, and its red tongue lolled from the rictus of its lips.

Several of the other beasts howled in response. One howled so loud and so pitifully that Brand wished he had never heard such a sound. It stood before him, shimmering silvery light all about it, and as though the light were fog that swirled and eddied, it seemed to rise higher on some invisible updraft of air.

But it was not air or fog. It was the beast itself. And when the swirling movement ceased, the beast was gone. What stood before him in its place was a Halathrin girl.

The girl seemed young, though she was an immortal and had perhaps walked the world since before the Camar had wandered out of the dim west as savages. Or she had been on the earth less than a score of years – he could not tell.

But he knew that she was beautiful. Her arms and body were covered by white samite. A soft hood was pulled up over her head, yet the shimmer from it paled beside the white-gold of her hair that spilled and escaped the confines of the cloth. Her eyes, above high cheek bones, were bright and keen, seeming one moment green and the next blue.

He stared at her, unable to take his gaze from the perfection of her skin or the nobility of her features. There was wisdom in her gaze, and pain. And both were deeper than the comprehension of his mind. But he saw anxiety there also, and anguish that tore at her soul however hard she strove not to show it.

When the girl spoke, she spoke in the language of the Halathrin. He knew it. He heard her words and understood them. It was the language of travelers all across the wide lands of Alithoras. And yet he had never heard it spoken like this. It seemed to him that anything he had heard before was like a blind man trying to describe how a day of high summer felt. But with her it was as though the warm sun shone and the green grass was soft beneath his feet and he could gaze through air so clear that he could see the red tongue of a bird gathering nectar from a flower across the other side of a valley. Summer was her very presence, and he felt it on his face and breathed it in with every breath.

"Forgive us," she said. And those simple words seemed to carry more meaning than a thousand words spoken by anybody else.

Tears from her bright eyes rolled down her high cheeks, but she made no move to wipe them away.

"We hunt. We must hunt. It is what we are made to do, and the devils inside drive us. We—"

The silver shimmer about her turned and twisted, suddenly becoming black. She raised her head and let out a tortured scream, and then she seemed to collapse to the ground. But she was gone, and the beast that Brand had seen first stood in the same place, its red tongue lolling.

He let out a long breath. His doubts were gone. The fate of the Halathrin was worse than death, for they understood what was happening to them but could do nothing to prevent it. Cardoroth might fall, might already have fallen, but Gilhain and Aranloth could not hold it against him that he came here to put an end to this. Kareste had been right.

But could she achieve what she had come here to do? And on what did she wait? For she stood silent and unmoving.

Brand did not know what would happen next, but it was the one thing he did not expect just at that moment.

There was a sudden flash of wings. A hawk darted through the air and screeched. The beasts looked at it.

Kareste looked at it, and Brand looked at it with a racing heart.

It landed, seeming to spear into the earth with a thump, but even before the wings ceased beating Durletha sprang up from the ground.

The witch stood between the two travelers and the beasts. She had taken the form of the old hag that Brand had first met her as, but her eyes were keen and bright.

Brand's heart raced even more, and it seemed that he could not stop it. A sudden fear overwhelmed him, and sweat coated his palms.

Now, of all times, the witch reappeared, and it was not by accident. This was not just a test of Kareste's power, but also a choosing of Light or Shadow, and Brand dreaded what evil the witch might be able to work in the midst of all that.

23. A Man is Judged by his Deeds

Shorty was prepared to die. He had put up a good fight, and whatever else happened he had bought some time for Brand. Every hour counted. Every hour Cardoroth survived was an extra hour his friend had to save them.

With a thrust of his jaw Shorty stopped his slow retreat. He might die today, but he had no intention of making it easy for Hvargil.

The traitor to the realm, who would be its king, advanced. He smiled coldly, but in truth he had nothing to be happy about. Whatever arrangement he had with the elùgroths now, he did not guess how quickly it would dissolve later. Lust for dominion had driven him and blinded his sharp mind to what it would be like to rule under the hand of the elùgroths. Promises would come easily to them now, but their words would be less than dust and ash if the winds of fortune blew victory their way.

"Time to die, little man. Did I not warn you? You should have fled when you could."

Shorty made no answer, but his eyes glinted with hatred.

Hvargil grinned at him.

"Will you pit bare hands against a Halathrin blade?"

Shorty did not hesitate.

"If I must."

Hvargil looked at him, still advancing very slowly, but it seemed that a shadow of doubt was on him, and he grasped at an idea that suddenly crossed his mind.

"Perhaps I'll show you mercy. Run. Run back to the gate now, and I'll let you live. Your life for the sacrifice of some pride. It's a fair exchange, wouldn't you say?"

Shorty made no move, and Hvargil slowed his advance even more.

"Maybe when I rule the city I was born to lead, eldest of the royal line that I am, I will need my own Durlin. If you survive the fall of the city, seek me out. This much I'll say, for a king always rewards valor – you have fought bravely."

Shorty thought, and he thought quickly. Not about serving Hvargil, he would never do that, but about why the offer of mercy was made. There was only one reason, and a lot of little things came together to serve it. Hvargil always wished to show himself worthy of being a king, to show himself as reasonable and to present himself as an alternative to Gilhain. He, by contrast to the real king, could afford to show mercy, whereas Gilhain, constrained by necessity, could only ask men to serve and die. By drawing attention to these things Hvargil hoped to undermine the will of the defenders to fight.

Shorty knew what he had to do. He had to fight to the last, fight against all odds, and come out victorious. It was a near impossible task, but it would dismay Hvargil and defeat the purpose of the whole challenge. Hvargil had guessed from the beginning that Gilhain would send a champion.

But Shorty smiled to himself. He liked a challenge. It made him feel alive. And looking at things in that light he realized that even dying, so long as he faced it with courage, would work in favor of bolstering the hearts of the defenders.

Shorty did what should never be done in a fight. He turned his back on the enemy. But he felt safe, at least for a few moments. Hvargil could not stab him in the back before all the defenders who looked on. That would only harden their resolve to fight.

Slowly, Shorty pointed to the battlement where the king stood, and he bowed to him long and deep. When he straightened, he loosed the cloth tied about his waist that bore the king's emblem, and he held it high.

Slowly, with a tight grin on his face, he turned to face Hvargil.

The man-who-would-be-king watched him. His jaw was clenched.

"A man is judged by his deeds," Shorty said, "and not by his height. And a king is judged by his loyalty to the people he rules. Kill me, traitor, if you can. But your gamble is already lost. In the eyes of those who defend Cardoroth, I will die as a hero, and they will oppose you, and those you serve, all the more."

Hvargil did not answer. But his face was a twisted thing beneath the beautiful helm, and he unleashed a furious attack.

Shorty retreated once again. As he stepped back he zigzagged randomly, making it hard for Hvargil to reach him. Agility combated brute strength, and it gave him time. But only so much. The Halathrin blade whirred through the air, always near and getting nearer.

So near the blade came that Shorty was indeed cut several times on his arms and hands. They were only nicks, and yet the white surcoat of the Durlin became blotched red with his blood.

Finally, Shorty saw his opportunity. Hvargil made yet another thrust, but this one was just a fraction too far.

It was not just for show that Shorty had taken the cloth belt of the king from his waist. He used it now, looping it around the blade, the fabric catching and tightening about the jeweled hilt.

With a great heave, using all his strength but applying it in one swift jerk, he pulled the blade from Hvargil's grip.

But he was not done. Even as the sword tumbled through the air he bounded forward and rammed his helm against the head of Hvargil. The other man was not ready for it. There was a mighty thump, for the blow hit Hvargil under the jaw and drove upward. His neck could not turn to diminish the force of the strike.

Hvargil staggered back. He was dazed, yet even so he drew a dagger. Shorty kicked it out of his hand. And then he unleashed his anger. For this was a man who had cost Cardoroth dearly.

With speed and agility he punched and kicked and struck a whirlwind of hammering blows at his opponent. Hvargil reeled away, and as he half turned Shorty managed to reef the helm from his head.

Drawn to that now vulnerable target that he had exposed, Shorty found renewed strength and struck with fury until Hvargil's face was cut and bleeding in many places.

Amazingly, Hvargil kept to his feet, trying to fight back. But a great right hook eventually caught him clean on the side of his head. His knees buckled. His legs gave beneath him like a felled tree, and he toppled to the ground.

Shorty stepped back a few paces and retrieved the Halathrin blade. It felt strange in his hand, but he walked forward again, discarding his own helm and placing the Halathrin wrought helmet on his own head. There he stood above Hvargil, the sword levelled at him as the other man tried to get up.

Anger flushed through Shorty again. His hand trembled, but he could not kill an unarmed man. He stepped away, and bent down to pick up the king's cloth that lay in the dirt. With a flourish, he held the belt high.

From the Cardurleth came a roar. And then it doubled, thundering down from the wall and rolling across the field. He had won.

But even so, it was not yet over. The enemy war drums beat loud. There was a sudden rush of elugs. A thousand of them raced across the field. Shorty stared at them.

Hvargil staggered up and swayed before him, and then he bent over and vomited. Somewhere behind him lay Shorty's own sword, the sword of his father, and he knew he would never hold that familiar hilt in his hand again.

Shorty turned and ran. There was no shame in doing so now. But the gate would never be opened in time, and even if that were possible, the defenders could not do it anyway. They could not risk the enemy seizing it, and holding it open long enough for the great horde behind to enter.

Shorty knew he would be torn to shreds, and no sortie would come out of the gate to save him. They could not risk that for one man, nor could he blame them.

He nearly ran anyway, for the instinct to live, if even only for a few moments longer, was strong. But instead, he bowed once more to the king.

When he straightened, he faced the onrushing enemy, raised his sword high, and planted his feet firmly on the ground.

Gilhain looked down with horror on the scene far below.

"Do something!" he said to Aranloth.

It was not a command. It was not a suggestion. There was an element of begging in his voice, and he did not care who heard it.

But the lòhren was already moving.

One of Aranloth's arms swept slowly out before him, palm down. Then, just as slowly, he turned the palm upward.

There was strain on his pale face, for whatever he did taxed him; it taxed him more than a man who was newly come back from near death should be taxed, but he did it unflinchingly. And he did it with a slow determination, the same slow determination and inhuman patience that had enabled him to face situations such as this before, to withhold his power until just that moment of maximum effect.

Gilhain looked at the racing elugs. They streamed across the ground like a river that had flooded its banks, and they raised their swords, yelling and cavorting as they sped, each one trying to be the first to reach their victim.

Gilhain looked at his champion. Shorty stood still as a standing stone, a stone that had been planted there for millennia. His sword was up, but his head was down. There was something in his posture that told Gilhain the man was not scared of death, and yet all the same he was filled with overwhelming sadness. For the end of his life was come, and he knew not what, if anything, would follow.

And then, transforming that sad scene, a wall of flame spurted from the ground. It leaped and danced and grew.

Shorty slowly straightened. The flame stood between him and the enemy. He hesitated a moment, but no more than that, and then he turned and began to walk back to the gate.

He did not hurry, and he took the time to point his sword at Aranloth upon the battlement. It might have been a salute. Or a thank you. Or a sign of respect, but whatever it was, it was a solemn gesture, and the lòhren returned it just as slowly, the flames dancing higher as his arm moved.

"Thank you," Gilhain said quietly. "If ever a man deserved to live, it's him."

24. I Must Drink my Fill

Brand did not take a backward step. He drew his sword, but he knew that battle could not get him out of this. What he needed was time, but no man ever had enough of that.

Already he sensed Kareste begin to focus her will next to him. Her head was bowed, and her hands held tight Shurilgar's staff.

The witch spoke. "Now is the time, Brand of the Duthenor. Choose death, or choose … something else."

"My choice was made long ago," he answered.

"Then you will die."

"Perhaps. But I doubt it."

She studied him. "So confident? It's a trait of the young, though I won't say you have no reason for it. But you have less now than usual, surrounded on all sides by enemies that overpower you."

"Not surrounded."

"Ha! You speak of Kareste, and you would buy her time for the enchantment she begins. But what enchantment? To free poor Halathrin souls? So much I discern that she has told you. And truly, it could only be done with one of the halves of Shurilgar's broken staff. And yet, brave fool, have you not thought what else could be done with the broken half she carries now? What she does even as we speak?"

Brand offered no answer.

"I will tell you, brave fool. She holds in her hands the same power by which the beasts were made. By it they can be released … or they can be *controlled*. She could make them her own creatures and be a force in the world, and with the staff in her possession it would just be the beginning."

He looked at Kareste. She now lifted her gaze upward. Her face was expressionless. Her ash-blond hair shimmered like the beasts. Her green-gold eyes glittered, filled with incalculable power. She looked resplendent, beautiful beyond words, but distant and terrible as implacable fate.

She did not look at him. She did not look at the witch. The wolf-beasts howled and the crows danced madly within the willows.

"Kill her now!" cried Durletha. "Or all that follows, the great Shadow that will spread across the land, will be your fault. Kill her now, while her mind is deep within her enchantment, or be condemned by all who loved and trusted you."

Brand gritted his teeth. No man could make such choices, and yet he caught a glimpse of the long life of Aranloth, the many such choices he must have made, and appreciated anew what he had given of himself for the protection of the land. And he appreciated also what a burden it was.

He shifted his grip on the Halathrin blade. It glittered blue-white beside the dark waters of the tarn that he was backed up against.

His gaze went to the witch. And then to Kareste once more. He had though the choice to be made was hers, had thought that she must choose either Light or Shadow. That was certainly true, but he must also choose, and the world had suddenly become far less clear-cut than he had thought.

Beyond the ever-present but rarely seen extremes of Light and Shadow was the place that men must live. And

171

what might be a dark deed to one was an act of heroism to another.

He did not know what to do, but after a moment he straightened.

A bitter brew you have mixed for me," he said to the witch. "But I came to the table when I agreed to this quest, and now I must drink my fill, for good or for ill."

She looked at him with hard eyes, and he thought that he detected a mixture of frustration and surprise in them. There was, perhaps, even admiration.

"Truly, you have a devil inside you. There's just no give. Do you know what you could achieve if only you set yourself free of constraints?"

Brand shrugged. He was happy to talk. It gave time to Kareste.

"There's no devil inside me. I'm just a simple man trying to do the right things for the people I love."

"Love will get you killed."

"And so might hate. Or greed. Or ambition. Or, for that matter, cowardice. And anyway, perhaps it's better to die trying to do right, than to live knowing you've done wrong. What do you think?"

The witch let out a long breath and gave a slight shrug of her bony shoulders.

"I think that you are not a simple man at all. But it does not matter what I think, anymore. Events have come to a head. I will have the staff now, even if I must kill you, for others come for it, and I *will* have it. It is easier to take it from her now than to wait and try to take it from them later."

Brand shifted slightly so that he stood between Kareste and the witch.

"For all your words, you still do not attack. I think you would prefer the beasts to do your work for you. But they make no move. They sense Kareste's enchantment

172

building, sense that she will set them free. Or can you not feel that?"

The witch turned slightly and her gaze darted to the beasts.

Brand had no idea if what he had said was true, but it sent a shiver of doubt through her, and it gave him the opportunity he was looking for.

Surprise was his friend, and he needed all the help he could get, for once Durletha turned on him, which she was about to do, he would be outmatched.

He had held the sword before him, but it was with Aranloth's staff that he attacked. He did not doubt that he had to use it, to draw on the power that was in him, for without his protection Kareste would die and the Halathrin would be trapped forever. He would deal with the consequences later.

Bright flame, blue-white, shot from the tip of the staff. It enveloped the witch, knocked her down and sent the beasts scattering to get away from her.

A moment she rolled on the ground, and then she was up, her eyes blazing. Her hand darted forward, fingers spread. Green flame dripped from them, and then it shot in a shimmering spray at Kareste.

Brand knew the attack was directed at her, even though he stood in the way, he felt it in the driving force of the flame; it struck him, but it mostly sought to get passed him.

He felt the heat of the attack, and the grass at his feet withered and blackened. Yet a blue-white nimbus had sprung up about his body, summoned by some reflex of his mind to protect him, and it expanded and shrank, stifling the green flame.

But the witch was not done. She raised her other hand and sent a second stream of fire at him.

Brand felt the force of it envelop him. The nimbus flickered, and he sank to his knees as though burdened with a weight beyond his strength to carry.

The green flames darkened, turning near black. He felt ever greater heat from them, and the blackened grass at his feet disappeared in smoke while the very earth itself began to seethe and bubble.

Brand thought of Cardoroth. He thought of Gilhain and Aranloth, of Shorty and Taingern. He thought of Arell.

He lifted his head. His eyes blazed. There was a free and reckless surge in his spirit. It was something that he had felt a few times before: the darker the hour, the greater the light within him shone. So it felt now. He staggered to his feet, and then he took a pace toward Durletha. And then another one. He found that with each step his strength seemed to grow.

Durletha looked at him, her eyes wide. The green flame sputtered and died.

"There *is* a devil in you," she said.

Brand took another pace forward, his staff held high in one hand, his sword in the other.

Durletha shook her head. "You make it hard for me to kill you, but courage is no match for skill. Of the first you have an abundance, of the latter—"

She did not finish that sentence. Instead, she made a quick gesture with her left hand. The fog that was all about them shuddered, and then like an arrow shot from a bow, it darted at Brand. As a wall it struck him, but it was no longer insubstantial.

The fog roiled and bubbled about him. It was become heavy as water, though it did not fall to the ground. Instead, it pressed in on him, forcing its way into his mouth and ears and eyes. He clenched his jaw and squeezed his eyes shut, but the water still drove into his nose.

He coughed and spluttered, lifting his arms to try to protect his face. He staggered toward Durletha, but she stepped nimbly away from him.

He could not breathe. Soon, he would choke and pass out. And then he was likely to drown, for already he felt the first specks of water in his lungs. That made him cough, but the moment he opened his mouth to do so, water forced its way in there, too.

He did what he did not wish to do: turn his back on Durletha. It left him even more vulnerable, and it did not stop the water as he thought it might. It followed him wherever he went, like someone with a pillow relentlessly trying to smother him.

He opened his eyes. The water rushed at them, yet through the rush he could still see a little of what was going on.

Kareste had not moved. She stood as she had done, but dark forces swirled around her. It was something that he sensed more than saw, and whatever she was doing occupied her completely. She could not help him, even if she wanted too. More, he sensed those dark forces reaching out to the beasts. She was binding them to her, joining with them, or the otherworldly power within them, and his heart sank.

Durletha may have been right in what she claimed before. Or not. Brand had no time to think, to get a true feel for what Kareste was doing. There was little time left for him, and he must soon discover a way out of the witch's trap, or die. Instinct had saved him the first time, but now, if he was to save himself again, he must draw on some knowledge or skill.

He fell to his knees. Not because he was quite incapacitated yet, but because it would assure Durletha that her attack was working. That might encourage her to just keep on going as she was. He did not need a knife in the back as well.

Out of the corner of his eye he saw some of the beasts. They howled, heads lifted up, snouts pointing to the sky, but he could hear nothing except the rush of water in his ears.

At least they were not attacking. Even if Kareste was binding them to her, it was helping him just at the moment. For if they attacked him now there was nothing he could do about it.

Blue-white fire still sputtered on Aranloth's staff. And where the rushing water touched it wisps of steam rose into the air. He stared at it, and then, dimly, an idea came to him.

He coughed and spluttered, feeling water reach his lungs, and with it a cold rush of heart-pounding panic. Yet he drew his will together and concentrated. It was harder than it had been before, much harder, for it was not instinctive. Yet the blue-white nimbus sprang to life about him once more.

This time he did not use it as a shield. Nor did he attack with it. Instead, he joined his thought with the water that surrounded him, and the lòhrengai he had summoned followed wherever his thought went.

Nothing happened. But he was not done. Having joined his lòhrengai with the witchery, he began to will the blue-white nimbus to grow hot. And hot it grew.

Steam sizzled through the air. Immediately he felt a lessening of the pressure of the water. He opened his eyes, stood, and faced Durletha.

He could not see her properly for all the steam and fog and light that surrounded him. But he saw enough to bring confidence to him. Her face showed surprise. She had thought him beaten, and he was not beaten. He stood taller.

The last of the water evaporated into the air. Still, he coughed, and each breath he drew felt as fire. Yet he looked at her with determination in his eyes, and he sensed her chagrin.

"Well," she said. "Aren't you just full of surprises? But I have the skill to play this game all day. Do you?"

He grinned at her. "Perhaps you do. But I know now that mine is the greater strength. Leave now, while you can. Give up the staff – it is not for you. It is a thing of the past, and it has no place in the world of today. Its evil *will* be destroyed."

"No," she said. "I'll have it. Though I don't see why you would try to stop me. What difference does it make to you if she has it," the witch pointed to Kareste, "or me? In either case, it will *never* be destroyed."

"But it will," he said. "The difference is this – I trust her. *She* will destroy it. And you never would."

"Fool!" Durletha hissed. "No one can wield such sorcerous power as she now does and not succumb to it. The staff will own her, if it does not already. Had you ever met its maker, had you ever met Shurilgar, you would know how great he was, and how strong his will. And his will lingers in the staff."

Brand winked at her. It was a gesture so out of place that it surprised her. And his following words threw her off balance even more.

"You know much, and you guess more. But you do not know all. When first I came to Cardoroth I met Shurilgar, or the spirit of him that haunted the dark woods of Lake Alithorin after his death. He turned his will upon me, and I survived. I defeated him, and set him wailing away in the dark. I do not fear him, and I fear you less. And as for Kareste—"

177

He ceased speaking and struck. All the while that he had been talking he had heard the crows caw and flap in the willows by the tarn. He took that sound and drew it together with his will, sending it as a spear at her.

Durletha flung up a haggard old arm, the rags she wore billowing with the sudden movement. But she moved with speed and confidence that bellied her looks. The driven sound struck her, sending her reeling back, but a shield of green flickered to life around her arm, and then she steadied herself and smiled at him. Her grin was gap-toothed. Her hooked nose twitched, and then she flung his own attack back at him.

But he was ready. With a wave of his sword, now flickering blue-white with lòhrengai, he knocked it to the side. The blade rang with a strange sound, and then he advanced.

Both sword and staff flickered with lòhrengai. She retreated. The beasts howled behind her. They trembled and shook and bit at their own tails. Whatever magic Kareste was working on them was having an effect, and he saw a glint of desperation in Durletha's eyes. She stopped her backward pacing.

Brand felt her thoughts reach out, out to somewhere behind him. He sensed the darkness of the deep tarn. Or did he sense *her* sensing the darkness of the tarn? Lòhrengai was a tangled web, but he had no chance to untangle it now.

Shadows flocked about him with a thousand wings. He perceived that her mind had taken the willow leaves and the black water and transformed them into this attack, this thing that pummeled and struck at him like a host of hawks, their wing-beats fierce slaps of shadow that shattered light into fragments and sent them spinning away until there was nothing but dark.

It was darker than the deepest cave. It was blacker than a moonless midwinter night. It was more shadowy than the dim flicker of long lost memories, and as memories could be lost, so too he began to lose a sense of where he was and what he was doing.

The will of the witch was on him – strong, soothing, blotting out all of the world except her own smothering thoughts. And she thought of death, and the long dark peace of the tomb.

As though from afar Brand heard the howl of a wolf. It brought back a fleeting image of Kareste, alone and imbued with eldritch power. Was she bending the beasts to her will, her first step in becoming a force of darkness on the earth? Or was she reaching out to them, becoming one with them so that she might break the sorcery that bound them?

Why should he care? The thought was overpowering. It was so much easier to drift back down into darkness. *But he did care.*

And because he cared, he fought. He struggled up as though he were at the bottom of the dark tarn itself, launching himself toward the surface. But he could not get there. That, he knew instinctively. No matter how hard he tried, he would never reach freedom. But if not that way, then how?

His mind drifted, and he saw many things. He saw the face of the usurper who now ruled the Duthenor, saw his father and mother holding hands, saw them dead, saw the moonlit night where he swore vengeance and struck fear through the usurper.

He saw his coming to Cardoroth, and Shorty and Taingern. And he saw Arell: quick-witted, skilled, quiet, brimming with compassion that she kept hidden. He saw Gilhain and Aurellin. He had learned from them all.

179

And he saw Aranloth. Older than the others, burdened by years beyond count and responsibilities so heavy that few men would have the will to bear them, and to endure their bearing, down through uncounted centuries. And he saw him atop the Cardurleth, sending his spirit into the elùgroth tent, worried that perhaps the task he had set himself would kill him and his soul be lost. He heard his words in the hollow dark that pressed about him. *Use your sword and prick my flesh, even to the point of drawing blood. That strengthens the tie between spirit and body, and should pull me back.*

Brand now knew what to do. Even as he thought of it he felt the hilt of the sword in his hand. It felt like a tongue of flame, and when he brought it to bear against his leg it whipped him with fire.

His eyes sprang open. The dark was gone. The world rushed upon him, brilliant and full of light and sound and life.

He stepped toward the witch. The sword in his hand burned, for he could fill it with lòhrengai just as easily as the staff.

Durletha looked at him. Surprise and fear was on her face. She began to shimmer, her arms lifting up, and he knew she was changing form.

Brand ran her through. The sword passed into her flesh as though nothing was there. The blade flared. Fire surged. Her arms dropped, and her body grew limp. It was heavy now, and it seemed to fall from the blade. She collapsed to the ground. Once she blinked, her hand reaching out to him. And then she who had endured as long, or perhaps even longer than Aranloth, died.

The Halathrin-that-were-wolves howled. The crows in the willows beat their wings in madness.

Brand reached down and with his palm closed Durletha's eyes. He had not wanted to kill her. But he killed her because he had to. Not just to save himself, or for Kareste, or for Cardoroth. But for all Alithoras.

He sensed now why he had the power that he did. He sensed that it came, as all power ultimately did, from the land, from whence he was born and to where he would one day return. He perceived his responsibilities and purpose, and did not know whether to shrink from them or embrace them. The second he was fearful to do, for it would change his life beyond the grasp of his imagination.

At least, he could not embrace it yet.

He turned to Kareste. The spell she wrought was at its peak. Shurilgar's broken staff was like a rent in reality. It was a thing of power, not truly belonging to this world, and it bridged the gap between this world and others. Nor did it belong to this time. It reached back into the distant past, sustaining itself on enchantments that were made long ago, and yet had not died with their maker. Shurilgar was gone, but his will lived on.

Force roiled through Kareste. Her ash-blond hair trailed in the wind, though no air moved. She shivered. And then she groaned. He could see that she was in agony. Or perhaps it was ecstasy. He could not be sure what she felt.

Suddenly, she stiffened. A wordless cry burst from her lips. She lowered the staff, and the power from it flickered and subsided.

The beasts howled again, and when he turned to look at them he saw that they were beasts no more. A score of Halathrin stood around him. There was anguish on their faces such as he had never seen.

There was a cry behind him, and he turned again. Kareste had fallen to her knees. Her head shook from side to side and she convulsed, her eyes rolling in her head, and then went still.

He ran to her. He turned his back to the Halathrin and ran. Kareste needed him, if it was not already too late. She needed him, and he would be there for her. Though what she would do if she recovered, he did not know.

Still less did he know what he would do if she died.

Thus ends *Defiant Swords*. The Durlindrath series will continue in book three, where Brand learns more of the threat to Alithoras and faces his greatest challenge yet.

Sign up below and be the first to hear about new book releases, see previews and learn of upcoming discounts. http://eepurl.com/Rswv1

Visit my website at www.homeofhighfantasy.com

Encyclopedic Glossary

Many races dwell in Alithoras. All have their own language, and though sometimes related to one another, the changes sparked by migration, isolation and various influences often render these tongues unintelligible to each other.

The ascendancy of Halathrin culture, combined with their widespread efforts to secure and maintain allies against elug incursions, has made their language the primary means of communication between diverse peoples.

For instance, a soldier of Cardoroth addressing a ship's captain from Camarelon would speak Halathrin, or a simplified version of it, even though their native speeches stem from the same ancestral language.

This glossary contains a range of names and terms. Many are of Halathrin origin, and their meaning is provided. The remainder derive from native tongues and are obscure, so meanings are only given intermittently.

Some variation exists within the Halathrin language, chiefly between the regions of Halathar and Alonin. The most obvious example is the latter's preference for a "dh" spelling instead of "th".

Often, Camar names and Halathrin elements are combined. This is especially so for the aristocracy. No other tribes had such long-term friendship with the Halathrin, and though in this relationship they lost some of their natural culture, they gained nobility and knowledge in return.

List of abbreviations:

Azn. Azan

Cam. Camar

Chg. Cheng

Comb. Combined

Cor. Corrupted form

Duth. Duthenor

Esg. Esgallien

Hal. Halathrin

Leth. Letharn

Prn. Pronounced

Age of heroes: A period of Camar history that has become mythical. Many tales are told of this time. Some are true, others are not. And yet, even the false ones usually contain elements of historical fact. Many were the heroes that walked abroad during this time, and they are remembered still, and honoured still, by the Camar people. The old days are looked back on with pride, and the descendants of many heroes yet walk the streets of

Cardoroth, though they be unaware of their heritage and the accomplishments of their forefathers.

Alar: *Azn.* A strain of horses raised in the southern deserts of Alithoras. Bred for endurance, but capable of bursts of speed. Most valued possession of the Azan people, who measure wealth and status by their number. In their culture, where a person on foot is likely to die between water sources, horse-theft is punished by torture and death.

Alithoras: *Hal.* "Silver land." The Halathrin name for the continent they settled after the exodus. Refers to the extensive river and lake systems they found and their appreciation of the beauty of the land.

Alith Nien: *Hal.* "Silver river." Has its source in the mountainous lands of Auren Dennath and empties into Lake Alithorin.

Anast Dennath: *Hal.* "Stone mountains." Mountain range in northern Alithoras. Contiguous with Auren Dennath and location of the Dweorhrealm.

Angle: The land hemmed in by the Carist Nien and Erenian rivers, especially the area in proximity to their divergence.

Angrod: One of the ancient names of the witch better known in present times as Durletha.

Arach Neben: *Hal.* "West gate." The great wall surrounding Cardoroth has four gates. Each is named after a cardinal direction, and each also carries a token to represent a celestial object. Arach Neben bears a steel ornament of the Morning Star.

Aranloth: *Hal.* "Noble might." A lòhren.

Arell: A name formerly common among the Camar people, but currently out of favor in Cardoroth. Its etymology is obscure, though it is speculated that it derives from the Halathrin stems "aran" and "ell" meaning noble and slender. Ell, in the Halathrin tongue, also refers to any type of timber that is pliable, for instance, hazel. This is cognate with our word wych-wood, meaning timber that is supple and pliable. As elùgroths use wych-wood staffs as instruments of sorcery, it is sometimes supposed that their name derives from this stem, rather than elù (shadowed). This is a viable philological theory. Nevertheless, as a matter of historical fact, it is wrong.

Aurellin: *Cor. Hal.* The first element means blue. The second appears to be native Camar. Queen of Cardoroth and wife to Gilhain.

Auren Dennath: *Comb. Duth.* and *Hal. Prn.* Our-ren dennath. "Blue mountains." Mountain range in northern Alithoras. Contiguous with Anast Dennath.

Azan: *Azn.* Desert dwelling people. Their nobility often serve as leaders of elug armies. They are a prideful race, often haughty and domineering, but they also adhere to a strict code of honor.

Barok: A healer in Cardoroth. A man held in high regard by the profession he represents. Distantly related to the king on his mother's side. It is believed by some that he obtained his position as chief physician via political influence. Others argue that, his family being wealthy, they bribed the king's chancellor in order to obtain the favored position for one of their own. Be that as it may, it is well known in Gilhain's court that the king dislikes him. This likely stems from an older cause, however. In his youth, the king required stitches. Barok inserted them, but miscalculated the date of their removal. The process, undertaken many days later than it should have been, was painful. Gilhain still bears the scars on his arm, not just of the initial cut, but also the faint point marks where the string was pulled from his flesh.

Brand: A Duthenor tribesman. Currently serving King Gilhain as his Durlindrath. However, by birth, he is the rightful chieftain of the Duthenor people. However, an usurper overthrew his father, killing him and his wife. Brand, only a youth at the time, swore an oath of vengeance. That oath sleeps, but it is not forgotten, either by Brand or the usurper. The usurper sought to have him killed also, but without success.

Bragga Mor: *Cam.* A great poet and storyteller from the city of Esgallien. He traces his ancestry back to the days when one of his forefathers served Conhain, that realm's first king, as both bodyguard and court bard. It is said that Bragga Mor is similarly skilled in both music and in sword play.

Camar: *Cam. Prn.* Kay-mar. A race of interrelated tribes that migrated in two main stages. The first brought them to the vicinity of Halathar; in the second, they separated and established cities along a broad sweep of eastern Alithoras.

Camarelon: *Cam. Prn.* Kam-arelon. A port city and capital of a Camar tribe. It was founded before Cardoroth as the waves of migrating people settled the more southerly lands first. Each new migration tended northward. It is perhaps the most representative of a traditional Camar realm.

Carangar: *Hal.* "Car – red, angar – outcrop of rock or something prominent that juts from the surface of the land or another object." A Durlin.

Cardoroth: *Cor. Hal. Comb. Cam.* A Camar city, often called Red Cardoroth. Some say this alludes to the red granite commonly used in the construction of its buildings, others that it refers to a prophecy of destruction.

Cardurleth: *Hal.* "Car – red, dur – steadfast, leth – stone." The great wall that surrounds Cardoroth. Established soon after the city's founding and constructed with red granite. It looks displeasing to the eye, but the people of the city love it nonetheless. They believe it impregnable and say that no enemy shall ever breach it – except by treachery.

Careth Nien: *Hal. Prn.* Kareth nyen. "Great river." Largest river in Alithoras. Has its source in the mountains of Anast Dennath and runs southeast across the land before emptying into the sea. It was over this river (which sometimes freezes along its northern stretches) that the Camar and other tribes migrated into the eastern lands. Much later, Brand came to the city of Cardoroth by one of these ancient migratory routes.

Carist Nien: *Hal.* "Ice river." A river of northern Alithoras that has its source in the hills of Lòrenta.

Carnhaina: First element native *Cam*. Second *Hal.* "Heroine." An ancient queen of Cardoroth. Revered as a saviour of her people, but to some degree also feared, for she possessed powers of magic. Hated to this day by elùgroths, because she overthrew their power unexpectedly at a time when their dark influence was rising. According to dim legend, kept alive mostly within the royal family of Cardoroth, she guards the city even in death and will return in its darkest hour.

Carnyx horn: The sacred horn of the Camar tribes. An instrument of brass, man high with a mouth fashioned in the likeness of a fierce animal, often a boar or bear. Winded in battle and designed to intimidate the foe with its otherworldly sound. Some believe it invokes supernatural aid.

Chapterhouse: Special halls set aside in the palace of Cardoroth for the private meetings, teachings and military training of the Durlin.

Crenel: The vertical gap on a battlement between merlons. The merlon offers protection, the crenel an opening through which missiles are fired.

Drùghoth: *Hal.* First element – black. Second element – that which hastens, races or glides. More commonly called a sending.

Durletha: *Hal.* "She who is as enduring as stone." A witch of Alithoras whose birth was before even the rise of the ancient, but now forgotten, Letharn empire.

Durlin: *Hal.* "The steadfast." The original Durlin were the seven sons of the first king of Cardoroth. They guarded him against all enemies, of which there were many, and three died to protect him. Their tradition continued throughout Cardoroth's history, suspended only once, and briefly, some four hundred years ago when it was discovered that three members were secretly in the service of elùgroths. These were imprisoned, but committed suicide while waiting for the king's trial to commence. It is rumored that the king himself provided them with the knives that they used. It is said that he felt sorry for them and gave them this way out to avoid the shame a trial would bring to their families.

Durlin creed: These are the native Camar words, long remembered and much honored, uttered by the first Durlin to die while he defended his father, and king, from attack. Tum del conar – El dar tum! Death or infamy – I choose death!

Durlindrath: *Hal.* "Lord of the steadfast." The title given to the leader of the Durlin.

Duthenor: *Duth. Prn.* Dooth-en-or. "The people." A single tribe, or sometimes a group of tribes melded into a larger people at times of war or disaster, who generally live a rustic and peaceful lifestyle. They are raisers of cattle and herders of sheep. However, when need demands they are fierce warriors – men and women alike.

Elugs: *Hal.* "That which creeps in shadows." A cruel and superstitious race that inhabits the southern lands, especially the Graèglin Dennath.

Elùdrath: *Hal. Prn.* Eloo-drath. "Shadowed lord." A sorcerer. First and greatest among elùgroths. Believed to be dead or defeated.

Elùgai: *Hal. Prn.* Eloo-guy. "Shadowed force." The sorcery of an elùgroth.

Elùgroth: *Hal. Prn.* Eloo-groth. "Shadowed horror." A sorcerer. They often take names in the Halathrin tongue in mockery of the lòhren's practice to do so.

Elu-haraken: *Hal.* "The shadowed wars." Long ago battles in a time that is become myth to the Camar tribes.

Erenian River: A river in northern Alithoras. Some say its name derives from a corruption of the Halathrin word "nien," meaning river. Others dispute this and postulate the word derives from a pre-exodus name adopted by the Camar tribes after they settled the east of Alithoras.

Exodus: The arrival of the Halathrin into Alithoras from an outside land. They came by ship and beached north of Anast Dennath.

Faladir: A city founded by a Camar tribe.

Foresight: Premonition of the future. Can occur at random as a single image or as a longer sequence of events. Can also be deliberately sought by entering the realm between life and death where the spirit is released from the body to travel through space and time. To achieve this, the body must be brought to the very threshold of death. The first method is uncontrollable and rare. The second exceedingly rare but controllable for those with the skill and willingness to endure the danger.

Forgotten Queen (the): An epithet for Queen Carnhaina.

Free Cities: A group of cooperative city states that pool military resources to defend themselves against attack. Founded prior to Cardoroth. Initially ruled by kings and queens, now by a senate.

Galenthern: *Hal.* "Green flat." Southern plains bounded by the Careth Nien and the Graèglin Dennath mountain range.

Gavnor: A lòhren of Queen Carnhaina's ancient court. Driven by desperate need he attempted to Spirit Walk, though he did not have sufficient skill. He saw deeply into what was, and what yet may be. But he was assailed. He had neither the skill to attempt to defend himself, nor to return to his body. He was lost in the void, from whence none had ever returned. Yet Carnhaina recalled him, revealing herself as a great power, greater than most lòhrens or elùgroths. But Gavnor was changed by the experience. He withdrew from the court, renounced his stature among the lòhren order, and wandered the land as a lover of nature. It is said that his power was increased, and he may well yet still live. But none have seen him for long centuries.

Gernlik: *Cam.* A Durlin.

Gilhain: *Comb. Cam & Hal.* First element unknown, second "hero." King of Cardoroth. Husband to Aurellin.

Graèglin Dennath: *Hal. Prn.* Greg-lin dennath. "Mountains of ash." Chain of mountains in southern Alithoras. The landscape is one of jagged stone and boulder, relieved only by gaping fissures from which plumes of ashen smoke ascend, thus leading to its name. Believed to be impassable because of the danger of

193

poisonous air flowing from cracks, and the ground unexpectedly giving way, swallowing any who dare to tread its forbidden paths. In other places swathes of molten stone run in rivers down its slopes.

Great North Road: An ancient construction of the Halathrin. Built at a time when they had settlements in the northern reaches of Alithoras. Warriors traveled swiftly from north to south in order to aid the main population who dwelt in Halathar when they faced attack from the south.

Grothanon: *Hal.* "Horror desert." The flat salt plains south of the Graèglin Dennath.

Halathar: *Hal.* "Dwelling place of the people of Halath." The forest realm of the Halathrin.

Halathgar: *Hal.* "Bright star." Actually a constellation. Also known as the Lost Huntress.

Halathrin: *Hal.* "People of Halath." A race named after a mighty lord who led an exodus of his people to the continent of Alithoras in pursuit of justice, having sworn to redress a great evil. They are human, though of fairer form, greater skill and higher culture. They possess an inherent unity of body, mind and spirit enabling insight and endurance beyond other races of Alithoras. Reported to be immortal, but killed in great numbers during their conflicts with the evil they seek to destroy. Those conflicts are collectively known as the elù-haraken: the Shadowed Wars.

Harakgar: *Leth.* The three sisters. Creatures of magic brought into being by the lore of the Letharn. Their

Harlak: *Leth.* An ancient name of Aranloth.

Harath Neben: *Hal.* "North gate." This gate bears a token of two massive emeralds that represent the constellation of Halathgar. The gate is also known as "Hunter's Gate," for the north road out of the city leads to wild lands full of game.

Hvargil: Prince of Cardoroth. Younger son of Carangil, king of Cardoroth. Exiled by Carangil for treason after it was discovered he plotted with elùgroths to assassinate his older half-brother, Gilhain, and prevent him from one day ascending to the throne. He gathered a band about him in exile of outlaws and discontents. Most came from Cardoroth but others were drawn from Camarelon.

Immortals: See Halathrin.

Karappe: A great healer of antiquity. Responsible for many of the medical treatises still used today among the Camar peoples. He lived to 109 years of age, and remained sprightly well past his hundredth birthday. Famous for recommending two mugs of beer, or one glass of wine, a day as good for health.

Kareste: A mysterious girl who helps Brand. She possess potent magic.

Kardoch: A hero of ancient lethrin society. Revered by them, and at times worshipped by them. It is believed that the elùgroths stamp out the latter practice. They have no room in their rule for reverence of anything save their own

195

power, and the power that they ultimately serve themselves.

Khamdar: An elùgroth. Leader of the host the besieges Cardoroth.

Kirsch: A race of men who established a mighty empire across Alithoras. Yet they predated even the Letharn and nearly all knowledge of them is lost forever.

Lake Alithorin: *Hal.* "Silver lake." A lake of northern Alithoras.

Letharn: *Hal.* "Stone raisers. Builders." A race of people that in antiquity ruled much of Alithoras. Only traces of their civilization remain.

Lethrin: *Hal.* "Stone people." Creatures of the Graèglin Dennath. Renowned for their size and strength. Tunnelers and miners.

Lòhren: *Hal. Prn.* Ler-ren. "Knowledge giver – a counsellor." Other terms used by various nations include wizard, druid and sage.

Lòhren-fire: A defensive manifestation of lòhrengai. The color of the flame varies according to the skill and temperament of the lòhren.

Lòhrengai: *Hal. Prn.* Ler-ren-guy. "Lòhren force." Enchantment, spell or use of arcane power. A manipulation and transformation of the natural energy inherent in all things. Each use takes something from the user. Likewise, some part of the transformed energy infuses them. Lòhrens use it sparingly, elùgroths indiscriminately.

Lòhrenin: *Hal. Prn.* Ler-ren-in. "Council of lòhrens."

Lòrenta: *Hal. Prn.* Ler-rent-a. "Hills of knowledge." Uplands in northern Alithoras in which the stronghold of the lòhrens is established.

Lornach: A Durlin. Friend to Brand and often called by his nickname of "Shorty."

Lost Huntress: See Halathgar.

Magic: Supernatural power. See lòhrengai and elùgai.

Menetuin: A city on the east coast of Alithoras. Founded by the Camar.

Merlon: The vertical stonework on a battlement between crenels. The merlon offers protection, the crenel a gap through which missiles are fired.

Netherwall: One of the ancient names of the witch better known in present times as Durletha.

Nudaluk: *Cam.* A bird of the woodpecker family.

Otherworld: Camar term for a mingling of half-remembered history, myth and the spirit world.

Red-fletched arrows: Cardoroth is famed for having great archers, and the greatest of them always use the red feathers of the Cara-hak turkey for their fletching. The bird is revered by them as a creature of luck, and it is considered ill fortune to shoot one. But many a farmer or hungry hunter does so, and the feathers are never wasted. But a wide variety of feathers are used from different bird species for arrow making, though all are dyed red before use.

Sellic Neben: *Hal.* "East gate." This gate bears a representation, crafted of silver and pearl, of the moon rising over the sea.

Sending: See Drùghoth.

Shadowed Lord: See Elùdrath.

Shazrahad: The Azan who commands an elug army, or serves as a lieutenant of an elùgroth.

Shorty: See Lornach.

Shuffa: A type of boat. Small, fast and ideal for travel by river. Favored by the villagers who dwell along the Careth Nien, and based on a design originating from ancient times when the Letharn fished the two rivers of the Angle. The same name is used in Cardoroth for a different kind of boat, slower and of a different shape. It's unclear which version is closer to the original design.

Shurilgar: *Hal.* "Midnight star." An elùgroth. Also called the betrayer of nations.

Sight: The ability to discern the intentions and even thoughts of another person. Not reliable, and yet effective at times.

Slithrest: One of the ancient names of the witch better known in present times as Durletha.

Spirit walk: Similar in process to foresight. It is deliberately sought by entering the realm between life and death where the spirit is released from the body to travel through space. To achieve this, the body must be brought to the very threshold of death. This is exceedingly dangerous and only attempted by those of paramount skill.

Sorcerer: See Elùgroth.

Sorcery: See elùgai.

Surcoat: An outer garment. Often worn over chain mail. The Durlin surcoat is unadorned white.

Taingern: *Cam*. A Durlin. Friend to Brand.

Tombs of the Letharn: The ancient burial place of the Letharn people. All members of the population, throughout the course of their long civilization, were laid to rest here. It was believed that to be interred elsewhere was to condemn the spirit to a true death, rather than an afterlife. The dead were preserved, and returned even from the far reaches of the empire. This was withheld from perpetrators of treason and heinous crimes. These were buried in special cemeteries near the river. Petty criminals were afforded an opportunity to redeem their place in the tombs on payment of a fine determined by the head-priest.

Tower of Halathgar: In life, the place of study of Queen Carnhaina. In death, her resting place. Somewhat unusually, her sarcophagus rests on the tower's parapet beneath the stars.

Unlach Neben: *Hal.* "South gate." This gate bears a representation of the sun, crafted of gold, beating down upon a desert land. Said by some to signify the homeland of the elugs, whence the gold of the sun was obtained by an adventurer of old.

War drums: Drums of the elug tribes. Used especially in times of war or ceremony. Rumored to carry hidden messages in their beat and also to invoke sorcery.

Wizard: See lòhren.

Wych-wood: A general description for a range of supple and springy timbers. Some hardy varieties are prevalent on the poisonous slopes of the Graèglin Dennath mountain range and are favored by elùgroths as instruments of sorcery.

From the author

I'm a man born in the wrong era. My heart yearns for faraway places and even further afield times. Tolkien had me at the beginning of *The Hobbit* when he said, ". . . one morning long ago in the quiet of the world . . ."

Sometimes I imagine myself in a Viking mead-hall. The long winter night presses in, but the shimmering embers of a log in the hearth hold back both cold and dark. The chieftain calls for a story, and I take a sip from my drinking horn and stand up . . .

Or maybe the desert stars shine bright and clear, obscured occasionally by wisps of smoke from burning camel dung. A dry gust of wind marches sand grains across our lonely campsite, and the wayfarers about me stir restlessly. I sip cool water and begin to speak.

I'm a storyteller. A man to paint a picture by the slow music of words. I like to bring faraway places and times to life, to make hearts yearn for something they can never have, unless for a passing moment.

www.ingramcontent.com/pod-product-compliance
Lightning Source LLC
Chambersburg PA
CBHW030324180626
46810CB00003B/1218